Trust in Love

By Melanie Adams

Trust in Love

First Print Edition: April 2019

Limitless Publishing, LLC
Kailua, HI 96734
www.limitlesspublishing.com

Formatting: Limitless Publishing

ISBN-13: 978-1-64034-576-8
ISBN-10: 1-64034-576-0

This is a work of fiction. Names, characters, places, and incidents either are the product of the author's imagination or are used fictitiously, and any resemblance to locales, events, business establishments, or actual persons—living or dead—is entirely coincidental.

Dedication

To everyone who has had their heart broken and found the courage to love again.

Prologue

Vancouver Island, 1997

The salty wind stung her little cheeks that day, that first time, whipping her hair into nasty knots. Grandma would have brushed them out, being careful not to tug too hard, but she had gone away in the night. Not the outside part, just the inside that makes you kind, funny, and gentle, that's how her momma had said it. Emma took her time finding the very best stick.

Grandma's room smelled like her baby sister's diaper, the first one in the morning. Her usual wrinkly warm hand was cold to the touch, too cold. Emma had covered her eyes with her hands, not wanting to see, peeking between her fingers because she couldn't stop. Grandma's skin had changed color to match the white pillowcase. She had whispered "Grandma" a few times, but she knew there would be no answer. She didn't know how she knew; she just did.

The stick etched out the words nicely into the

grey wet sand. The waves would soon reach them, carrying them out to the ocean angels. She hurt deep inside her chest, but she didn't cry; it would be too hard to see. Momma had said you couldn't see the angels, but maybe Momma wasn't looking hard enough.

I love you
I will be a good girl
Promise

Chapter One

When you least expect it, love barges in.

Present Day

The smallest twinge of jealousy pinched Emma's throat as she shifted into first, inching her way up the sloping driveway. The sandbox filled with brightly colored toys and the vacant swing set mocked her. A meticulously renovated country home perched on a rolling hill, the Pacific Ocean the backdrop and, of course, the white picket fence. A picture-perfect setting for the picture-perfect family. Her little sister had it all. A man who absolutely adored her, a healthy beautiful daughter, and a career well underway. Their mother would have been so proud of the woman Amy had become.

Reaching over the gate, she clicked open the metal latch as a fall wind thick with the chill off the ocean pulled at her sweatshirt. She shivered, groaned, and quickened her pace. The wind snatched the dry brittle leaves from the apple trees' twisted old branches and flung them in the air. Nature was restless, and Emma could easily relate. If her prince didn't show up soon, her ovaries would be dry, brittle, and covered in dust. He certainly was taking his sweet time.

Muffled laughter and screams from what sounded like a hundred small children leaked from the house. Easing the front door open just a crack, the volume shot up to ear-piercing level. Tiny bare feet slapped the hardwood floor at break-neck speed. Glorious smells flooded her nose—pepperoni pizza, chocolate cake, and, if her nose wasn't mistaken, a batch of their mother's famous buttery, fluffy, salty parmesan breadsticks. The handful of helium-filled balloons she had wrestled into her tiny car now pressed to the ceiling. Kicking off her shoes, she pushed them to the side, then twisted her waist-length locks into a knot and secured it with an elastic. The dull thud still tugged at the back of her head. She hoped the two aspirin kicked in soon.

A mass of screaming and bouncing four-year-olds rounded the corner and caught sight of Emma and the balloons. The entire group giggled and begged for a balloon all at the same time as Emma handed them out, saving the biggest, brightest one for the birthday girl.

She squatted in front of her niece with outstretched arms. "Happy birthday, sweet stuff."

Jessie's angelic face beamed with delight as she launched herself into Emma's arm, almost toppling Emma's slender frame backward, her floral dress as soft as a rose petal. She was a tiny carbon copy of her mother—delicate features, cherry red lips, and the most striking green eyes.

"Aunty Em." Jessie clung to her neck, giggling and wiggling while Emma tickled her ribs, bringing on a round of belly laughter.

She held Jessie tight to her chest. "I love you, sweet stuff."

Jessie planted a sticky chocolate kiss on Emma's lips. "I love you."

She wiggled herself free and took off running back to her friends. Tightly wound golden ringlets bounced with each step, the balloon bumping off the ceiling and walls. Emma picked herself up off the floor and turned into the kitchen.

Amy was scrambling to wipe up a puddle of grape juice before it rushed under the base of the fridge. She sat back on her heels, bundling the dripping mess of purple paper towel, and brushed her hair out of her face with the back of her hand. "Who knew a handful of tiny people could take over a house in such a short time? I'm glad you're here."

Emma offered a hand to help Amy to her feet. "I wouldn't miss it for anything."

"Dad can't make it. He called this morning, something to do with work. He's going to swing by later with Jessie's gift." Amy closed the garbage can lid with a bang.

"He tries, Amy, he really does." She pulled her in for a hug. "He'll be by later to enjoy a little quiet cuddle with Jessie."

"I know, I just wish he was around more, you

know?" She leaned into the hug, squeezing Emma a little tighter. "Mom's been gone a long time, almost fifteen years. He shouldn't be alone. It's not like he has to be. It's not good for him." She held Emma at arm's length. "Neither should you."

Emma pulled away and started backing out of the room. "I'm going to find that husband of yours. Sounds like the distinguished doctor is running a pony ride in the living room."

Amy waved her off. "You can run, but you can't hide. I'm not giving up, Emma."

Colorful streamers hung from the ceiling, spinning and bouncing, keeping pace with the circus below. Antique furniture was shoved to the side to make room for the rodeo. Two wild-eyed girls running on a sugar overload perched on Mike's back and clung to his white collared shirt, squealing, "Giddy-up." Half a dozen more ran in circles, repeatedly screeching, "Me next!"

Emma dropped to her hands and knees and whinnied. Small, sticky fingers brushed across her cheek and locked together under her chin, and the rodeo was on. Mike shot her a wink and a smile to say thanks, his disheveled appearance the trademark of a dad in full entertainment mode. She pranced and bucked around the room until her knees ached before dropping to her belly on the throw rug, succumbing to tickle monster duties.

A few rounds of musical chairs, then hide and seek, and the party finally wound down. With the last little guest exiting with her mother, and Amy upstairs bathing Jessie, it left Emma and Mike on clean-up duty. Mike cleared his throat, and Emma knew what was coming next; he rarely missed an opportunity. She knew a constant needling from her sister was the force behind it.

"How are things with you, Emma? Seeing anyone new?" he asked.

She turned and bent to pick up a fist full of toys while avoiding eye contact. "Things are good, busy with work."

Mike moved around the room, occasionally glancing over at Emma. He ran his fingers through his hair and opened and closed his mouth twice before he spoke. "There's a buddy of mine I've known since med school."

She turned to face Mike. "Do you recall the last blind date you sent me on?" She poked at her chest. "I certainly do. The gum in my hair, the nasty boat that stunk of dead fish and diesel, the completely out-of-control twin boys, and to top it off, the tumble into the harbor that resulted in the trip to the emergency room." She leaned forward and parted her hair to expose the scar. "You did a great job, by the way. The scar is barely noticeable." Emma dropped into a chair and stroked the silky material of Jessie's favorite stuffed animal. "I feel like I'm done with blind dates. I feel like the next one might be the end of me, literally."

"Emma, I'm sorry. Honestly, when he said he was taking you out for seafood, I thought he meant the restaurant." He shook his head, grinning. "Did I tell you he figured the date went pretty good and was going to call you in a few days?"

Emma threw her head back and laughed. "What did you tell him?"

"I said you're allergic to seafood." He tossed a stuffed toy at her. "Listen, Emma. I would drop this if it was just a set-up, but it's not. Brent's a good guy, a good friend. He lost his wife about a year ago. Actually, his concern is for his daughter. She's having a tough time. He needs someone special, and I mentioned your name. I hope you don't mind. I know you're busy, but if you could do this for me, as a favor. You're the best."

This wasn't exactly the usual setup; it was work related. But she could read between the lines.

Emma raised her hands to surrender. "Thank you for saying that. You know I'll do whatever I can."

Mike sat on the arm of the couch and folded one of Jessie's tiny sweaters in his lap. "Cancer took her, his wife. It happened pretty quickly. I can't imagine, Emma, losing your sister." He brushed his hand across the tiny sweater, his thumb circling the delicate pink button. "I don't even want to think about it. Brent seems okay, from what I can tell anyway, but his daughter has him concerned. She's eight, I believe. So young to lose your mother! But you know how it feels. I would really appreciate it if you would call him, feel things out. Besides, you never know where it might end up."

There it was, even if he tried to make it sound like it was only an afterthought. "What exactly do you mean, 'where it might end up'?" Emma asked.

Mike went digging through the front pockets of his pants, rattling out a small piece of white paper. "I told him I would give you his number."

She furrowed her brow. "Mike, answer me, what did you—?"

He cut her off as he took her hand, pressing the paper into her palm. "Here's his number. I really appreciate this, Emma."

She chuckled, looking down at the prescription paper with the name Brent Davies written across the top.

Mike grinned. "What?"

Waving the prescription paper in the air above her head, she giggled. "Is this the only paper you could find to write on or are you prescribing men now?"

"Emma, you are my favorite sister-in-law. If a prescription is what you've been waiting for, consider it done."

"Never mind being your favorite, I'm your only sister-in-law." She stared at the paper. "Wouldn't it be great if it were that easy?"

"So, call. He's a good guy who needs some healing time; and besides, maybe it will be that easy."

"That's twice now, insinuating it could lead somewhere. Are you up to something? Is there something I should know?"

This time, he avoided her stare by getting back to cleaning.

"Seriously, Mike." She tossed the stuffed toy back at him. "Is there an ulterior motive here?"

"Would it be that bad?" Mike asked.

Rarely a day went by that she wasn't eagerly waiting for her dream man, for love. It was all necessary to live life, to make it life, she knew that. The fact she couldn't make anything last was also a certainty. One so-called normal man after another, one reason for running after another.

"Mike, I'm grateful you and Amy have an interest in my love life. I know you mean well, but I just think it will happen when the time is right."

"I don't think there's any harm in helping time hustle it up. You deserve a good guy." He pulled her in for a gentle hug, which turned into one of his famous bear hugs.

She succumbed to the welcome embrace. "I will be fine, just you watch."

A knock at the door broke the hug. "Emma, would you mind getting that?"

"Of course, it's probably Dad. Amy will be happy." She crossed the room and swung the door open. "Oh, hello."

He stood there, one hand shoved deep inside his jeans, the other gripping a brightly colored gift box. A full head of dark hair buzzed short. Her imagination spun like a top. The same vision whirled over and over in her head. How nicely her arms would drape over his broad shoulders, his hands pressed to her back, pulling her to his chest. A long, passionate, intoxicating kiss, slipping her tongue past the row of perfect white teeth. The five o'clock shadow rough on her cheek.

"Hello." He offered the gift to Emma. "I just thought I'd stop by quickly and drop off a gift."

His voice washed over her. It felt like her insides were filled with sweet, thick molasses. She stepped to the side, fussed with ringlets that had broken loose, her cheeks burned, and not a single word passed her lips.

Mike placed a hand on Emma's shoulder. "Brent,

great timing, come on in. I wasn't sure you were going to make it. You got time for a beer? I know I'm ready."

"Yes, I could use a cold one." He offered his hand to Emma. "You must be Emma. Mike said you were beautiful, and that was an understatement." His warm callused hand dwarfed hers.

"I, thank you, yes…sorry, what did you ask me?" She stepped backward onto Mike's foot. "Oh, sorry, Mike. I'll go grab those beers. Excuse me." She turned quickly, stumbling, and almost ran into the wall. "First day, new feet." Her nervous giggle faded as she rounded the corner into the kitchen none too soon. She leaned against the kitchen counter, closed her eyes, and the ridiculous grin suddenly became awkward.

Locking her fingers around the neck of three beer bottles, she paused for a second or two. She soaked up the sound of his voice on the other side of the wall. Imagining those same lips brushing across her ear, her collar bone, a trail of kisses leading to her breast. The warmth of his mouth on her nipple sending goose bumps rushing across her skin. The two of them, naked, sweaty, and tangled in crisp white sheets.

She closed her eyes and focused on getting her thoughts back to reality. The furniture was back in place, and she handed Mike and Brent their beer and pressed hers to her cheek for a second or two before twisting off the cap. She sat on the edge of the chair, leaning forward, resting on her elbows. The two were deep into a conversation about the hospital and the need for new equipment. They went on about an x-ray, or a fundraiser, or was it ultrasound? It didn't matter. She looked down at her knee sticking out of her jeans and crossed her legs. She spotted chunks of chocolate cake ground into the cuff on the sleeve of her tattered old sweatshirt. One pink and one blue sock glared up at her. She whipped them both off, only to show a battered pedicure, three toes missing polish altogether. She tugged the elastic out of her hair; it tumbled around her face, the silky brown curls unwinding down her chest. When she glanced up, Brent's beautiful blue eyes locked on hers, a sideways grin lighting up his face.

Chapter Two

Sometimes love comes in gently, and other times it comes crashing in like a tornado, twisting up all the pieces of your life you had so painstakingly organized.

Emma's mind had been consumed since the not-so-chance meeting at Mike and Amy's. Brent had somehow become the main character in almost every thought she had. She took two wrong turns before finding their street. The road weaved between the old growth firs, giving the impression it was more of a meandering trail. Perfectly trimmed hedges, walls of rhododendrons, wrought iron gates, each address with its own special inviting entrance. She slowed to a stop when she spotted the house with the carved wooden grizzly bear holding the salmon in its paw. It was an impressive piece of art.

She bent the rear-view mirror in her direction for one last inspection and ran her fingers through her hair a couple of times. There was no harm in looking her best. Pulling her lip gloss out, she made a quick lap around her mouth and smiled wide to make sure nothing was in her teeth. Cupping her hand in front of her mouth, she huffed out a breath, still minty fresh.

Her hair whipped at her cheeks. Foaming green waves rolled up the beach, smashing them into a fine mist smelling of salt and seaweed. She shivered. Prickly bumps rushed every inch of her flesh.

Brent touched her shoulder, startling her. “Oh my, I didn’t hear you coming.”

“It’s cool today. I started a fire to take the chill off the house. Come on in and warm up. You can watch the ocean from inside.”

She turned to follow him, her gaze lingering on the view. “It is absolutely incredible here. You are so lucky.”

“I wouldn’t call it luck, more like a lot of hard work got us here. It was something Melissa and I both wanted. Walking the beach was one of our favorite pastimes, so we figured we may as well live here.”

Emma crossed her arms over her chest and shivered. “The beach is my favorite place, too.”

Together they crossed the wooden deck, which ran the full length of the log house and was lined with giant clay pots holding shrubs that had grown up bent by the wind. Grasping the long wooden handle, Brent opened one of the two oversized rustic wooden doors. Reaching behind her, his hand fell into place in the small of her back, gently guiding her inside. She swore she could feel the heat where they connected through her sweatshirt. She intentionally moved slowly, holding onto the connection as long as she could. Warm dry air rushed her cheeks. He slid his hand up her back, resting it between her shoulder blades.

Brent pointed to the chairs near the fireplace, “Please, make yourself comfortable. I made coffee. We can discuss things before Hope gets home from school.”

She kicked off her shoes and headed straight for the crackling fire. The unfinished wooden mantel was heavy with treasures, rocks, seashells, tangled smooth driftwood, and beach glass. “I see someone has been busy collecting.” She sank into the overstuffed brown leather chair, curling her legs underneath her.

“Melissa and Hope walked the beach almost every day. There is a giant pile of treasures out by the woodshed. You hungry? I can dig something up.” He opened the fridge and scanned its contents. “Pickles, yogurt in a tube, grape jelly. Wow, I need to hit the grocery store.” He swung the door shut.

“No thank you. I do love a good yogurt tube, but I had lunch not too long ago.”

Brent handed Emma her coffee. “This should help heat things up.”

Her hand brushed the top of his large, thick fingers. “Yes, thank you.”

Things were heating up all right, but it wasn’t just her hands. She cleared her throat. “You have a lovely home. I would love to see the rest.” She would also love to see him bringing her a cup of coffee—completely naked. Better yet, completely naked with a tray of fresh strawberries, two glasses of wine, and those big strong hands eager to explore every inch of her.

"If you are hungry, I just remembered I have some strawberries," Brent offered.

"*Oh yes.*" Her cheeks warmed. "No, no. I mean no, thank you. Unless they're chocolate covered, that's my favorite."

"Sorry, no chocolate. Wish I did." Brent eased himself into the matching chair and leaned back. "I'm glad you came. I was afraid you might decide Hope and I were more work than you wanted and change your mind about coming."

"Why would you think that?"

"I'm asking a lot, having you drive out here to see Hope. I really appreciate it."

"I don't mind one bit. The view alone would keep anyone coming back."

The corners of his mouth curled slightly as he glanced out at the water over his shoulder and then back at her. "I must agree, although the view inside is better with you here."

"Flattery will get you everywhere. Now, how about showing me the rest of the house?"

He stood and offered his hand to help her up from the chair. She slipped her fingers across his palm, and her insides couldn't decide if they were soup or fireworks. If he pulled her to his chest, kissed her hard, slipped one hand under her sweater, grazing his fingers across her flesh as he inched his way toward her breast, she wouldn't stop him. She pressed her fingertips to her temple. The thoughts weren't right; she needed to gain some control.

Work, she was here for work.

Emma dropped her sights to the floor. "This is beautiful. What kind of wood is that?"

Brent looked down at the floor, sliding his sock back and forth. "Reclaimed timber from the old church."

Of course, it's from the church, and he's a widower, and she is about to meet his daughter in need of a grief counselor, and her mind is crammed with dirty sexy thoughts. She wondered if it was normal to be thinking about kissing him as he spoke to her. His lips looked so inviting.

"It's beautiful; it must have taken a while."

Turning, he waved for her to follow him. "It did, but it was worth it. I also mastered the skill of tiling."

Emma followed. "Tiling, wood flooring, what don't you do?"

Glancing back at her over his shoulder, he continued down the hall. "I had a lot of summer jobs to help pay for med school."

She fought the burning desire to let her eyes wander down to the backside of his tan cotton pants. It was her first day, after all. Getting caught admiring his extraordinary behind would be an embarrassing moment that would haunt her longer than she cared to imagine. The fight was lost halfway across the room, but who could blame her? So much for control.

She scanned the family portraits lining the hall, the first being Brent and Melissa's wedding. In all the other photos, their daughter sat between them. "The pictures are lovely. She was a beautiful woman. Hope looks just like her. A cross between Marilyn Monroe—young Marilyn, before Hollywood—and Jane Fonda. A classic healthy beauty."

Brent cocked his head to the side. "Two very beautiful actresses not from our generation."

"My dad loves the old movies. We both do. We get together once a week for movie night at his place."

"Maud Adams." He brushed a lock of hair over her shoulder, his finger grazing her cheek. "That's who you remind me of." He smiled. "I like old movies too."

"A James Bond fan. *The Man with the Golden Gun*, '74, I believe." She leaned against the wall, struck her best sexy pose, and lowered her voice an octave or two. "Can I get you a drink?"

He leaned against the wall a foot away, hooked a finger under her chin, and tilted her face up to meet his stare. "A medium dry vodka martini, slice of lemon peel, shaken not stirred."

"You make an excellent James Bond." Her voice was stuck in a sexy tone.

He brushed his thumb across her bottom lip. "Will you be my leading lady?" He caught sight of his watch. "Oh. We really should get going. I like to be waiting when Hope gets off the bus."

She eagerly followed him to the door, and he offered her a warmer coat for the walk, which she gladly took him up on. She found herself swimming in his heavy plaid jacket. Flipping the collar up to keep her neck warm rustled the scent of his cologne. She had no idea what kind it was, just the fantastic smell of Brent. She tucked the collar in closer to her nose and inhaled until she couldn't take in another ounce, holding it inside before slowly and reluctantly releasing it from her chest.

Brent shoved his hands in his pockets, looking up at the maple trees.

"Fall is here. Melissa loved fall. She would rake the leaves, and Hope jumped into the piles."

Emma stopped and picked up a crispy brown and yellow maple leaf, running her finger along the veins poking out like the back of an old woman's hands. They had always brought her grandmother to mind.

Brent's steps slowed. "I think about doing that kind of stuff with Hope, but then I don't want to remind her of her mother at every turn. She was such a happy kid, laughing all the time. I know she misses her mother, but I thought by now I would see her smile more often. I try, but I find most of the time I'm forcing my own smiles. I want to do whatever it takes to make my little girl feel real joy again."

"That's why I'm here. I wish my dad had found someone for all of us to talk to after Mom died, but it wasn't something his generation did." She knew her father loved her and Amy more than anything in the world, but he came from a different time and probably had no idea how to seek help. "It felt like my father had gone that same day. His shell continued to breathe and go through the motions of life. But it wouldn't have hurt for Dad to do some talking, too."

"I'm fine, Emma. I'm handling it." He shoved

his hands into his pockets and turned to face the road.

The bus slowed to a stop at the end of the driveway, the doors clanged open, and Hope jumped to the ground. She half smiled and hugged Brent's waist.

Brent kissed the top of her head. "How was your day, sweetheart?"

"Good, Daddy." She took Brent's hand and looked up at Emma.

"I have someone I want you to meet. This is Emma." He stepped behind Hope, resting his hands on her shoulders. "You remember we discussed finding someone for you to talk to about your feelings. She's here for you to talk to about what makes you sad."

"It's nice to meet you, Hope," Emma said.

Hope stared at Emma without saying a word.

Brent took her backpack from her. "How about we throw this inside and go for a walk on the beach?"

Hope smiled up at her dad. "Just you and me?" The smile faded. "Or is she coming?"

Brent stopped and gently turned her by the shoulders. "I know this isn't what you think you need, but I'm the parent, so I get to decide. Emma is here to help, and I'm sure if you gave her a chance…for me. Can you do it for me?"

Hope stepped back and rolled her eyes. "I guess."

Brent looked at Emma and mouthed the words, "I'm sorry."

Emma smiled. "It's okay."

***

Hope walked a few steps ahead, dragging a stick through the sand.

Emma caught up to her. "Hope, can I borrow your stick…just for a minute?" She started scratching out words in the sand. "My mother passed away when I was just a little older than you."

Miss you, Mom.
Love E.

Emma turned to Hope and offered her the stick. "When I was little, my mother told me that if you write a note in the sand, the waves will take it away. Words of love, sadness, hope, joy, float across the water to where the ocean and sky meet." Emma bent close to Hope's ear and pointed out across the open water. She softened her voice to almost a whisper. "The ocean angels collect the notes and take them to heaven."

Emma stood beside Hope, the two staring out across the water.

"After that, I never left the beach without writing a note. Would you like a turn?"

Hope took the stick and stared at Emma. "What can I write?"

"Anything you want. It's your note."

Hope bent and pressed the tip of the stick into the sand.

Mommy come home.

With the last line drawn, Hope skipped backward to keep her feet dry from the wave. It crept its way up the last few inches then turned, taking the note away.

She dropped the stick and turned to ask Emma, "When do you think she will get my note?"

She stood beside Hope and looked out over the water. "If I remember correctly, my mother said it only took a moment or two. I bet your mother liked the note and wishes she could come home too."

Hope picked up the stick and scratched out another note.

Daddy is sad.

Three powerful words. Emma wondered if Brent caught the importance.

Hope stood before Emma. "Can we do this every day?"

Emma smiled. "We can do this whenever you want."

Hope turned toward the house and started walking, her step a little lighter. "Good."

When Hope was no longer within earshot, the conversation took a more serious tone.

Brent offered Emma his arm for the walk back, a peaceful smile on his face. "Writing a note in the sand, interesting."

She tucked her hand in the crook of his arm. "My mother took me to the beach so I could write to my grandma. I missed her so much after she passed away. I was eight when she died suddenly, a heart attack. I found her that morning, in her bed."

“I’m sorry that happened to you.”

“It’s okay. To be honest, I think the day of the funeral was much harder. People coming and going from the house, bringing food, crying, sharing stories, more crying. The graveyard, looking at the casket and wondering if they had put her favorite blanket in there with her so she wouldn’t be cold.”

“I was there when Melissa passed. I crawled into the hospital bed with her and wondered if it would be the last time I felt her next to me. The last time I would feel her silky hair against my cheek, her tiny frame close to my chest. I listened to her breath. I’m not a religious man, but I found myself begging for a deal. I would have given my life. We had talked about how I was going to handle the boyfriends, and birthday parties, and every holiday she wouldn’t be around for. What we didn’t talk about was how the hell I was going to keep getting out of bed each day without her.” He looked out at the ocean for a moment or two. “I must have told her I loved her a million times.” His voice caught in his throat. “Not that night. She dozed off and I didn’t want to wake her. A few hours later, she stopped breathing—she was gone, and I just held her, telling her over and over I loved her.”

“She knew.” She squeezed his arm. “She knew.”

Brent scrubbed his hand across the top of his head. “The note in the sand…it had an impact on Hope. I have a gut feeling this is going to work out. You thinking the same thing?”

Emma nodded her head. “I was thinking the same thing. She’s an amazing girl, very bright.”

“If that is the beginning of things to come, Hope

and I got lucky." He cupped his hand over hers.

Her breath caught in her throat, putty, complete and utter putty.

Chapter Three

Death didn't concern itself with your desires, your plans, or your future, it just stepped in and snatched people from your life.

The space heater hummed, struggling to warm her office. An old building tucked in the back corner, enough room for a small desk, small couch, and the television. Brent was at the hospital right next door. She leaned back in her chair, grinning. Brent rushed in her mind once more. His powerful arms pulled her close, pressing her to his muscular chest, kissing the nape of her neck, his warm breath tickling her ear as he confessed his undying love for her. Since it was her fantasy, Brent swept her into his arms and carried her to the bed in the grass hut on the beach. He spent the rest of the day satisfying her every need. Four o'clock she would be pulling into their driveway, when her only concern would be Hope.

Two quick raps on the door let her know Nathan

had arrived. A tall, lanky, red-haired teenager slumped across the room before dropping to the couch. His hands remained shoved to the bottom of his pockets.

"Hey, Miss Black." His shoulders rolled forward, and the corners of his mouth sagged.

"Hey, Nathan." She dropped down beside him and handed him the wireless game controller. "I'm up for a good car race. How about you?"

He shrugged his shoulders. "Sure, whatever you're into."

A backyard drowning, a terrible tragedy, an accident. A ten-year-old boy almost drowned trying to save his four-year-old sister. The gate had been left open by the pool cleaning service. It all happened in a few brief, sickening moments. The local newspaper had all the facts and for the last three years since the accident printed reminders to keep your children safe. It was the anniversary today, and the paper didn't miss a beat.

"It should have been me." He ground the heel of his hand into his eye socket.

"I can understand where that's coming from." She wasn't sure if he was crying but wasn't about to look—it would have sent him bolting from the room.

His car lapped hers for the second time. "You sleeping behind the wheel, Miss Black?"

"No, I'm not sleeping, I think I picked the wrong car." She waved the controller around in the air like she was actually driving.

"That's *not gonna* help. Oh! Oh! Look at that, passing you for the third time. You might *wanna step* on it." His hands gripped the controller, his fingers moved like lightning. "She was good, like really good, not like me." He brushed his cheek quickly with the back of his hand. "I don't mean like in the pool that day. I just mean if one of us had to die, it should have been me."

Emma heard the catch in his voice, and it pulled hard at her heart.

"Did you know that how you are thinking happens so often they have even named it? It's called survivor's guilt."

"Whatever." He shrugged again.

"I think we all have someone we would give our life for, but we don't get to choose." *Game Over* flashed across the screen. "Give me another try?"

"I wish it was like the game; you screw up, so what, you just try again." He set the controller on the couch beside him, leaned forward, and dropped his face into his hands.

"What do you think you could have done differently?"

"*I dunno*! Found her sooner, carried her inside the house instead of just *sitting* there and *yelling* for *Mom*." He banged a fist on his leg. "I was a shitty big brother."

"Your parents have told me they're proud of you. You did the best you could do."

"Yeah, well, my best wasn't good enough. You still want another race?" He leaned back and picked up the controller.

"I'm game if you are. You'd better watch your rear-view mirror 'cause I'm coming for you."

Her mind wandered to Brent. She could fantasize

all she wanted, but that was as far as it would go. Brent was completely off-limits. Hope was her main focus. It would take time to see a clear picture of where she was in the grieving process. Nathan was the reminder she needed to stay focused, no distractions.

Chapter Four

Chasing love was exhausting. It couldn't be caught, trapped, or pinned down, it could only happen when the time was right.

If determined to behold the wonder of love you must prepare for pain.

Sooner or later it is inevitable.

Her friends were all married now, busy building their own lives, their own families. She had been a bridesmaid so many times she could open a store with all the tacky dresses hanging in her closet. She was tired of finding the wedding invitations in her mail and seriously wondered if being an old maid was her future.

It was certainly reasonable to want a man and love and romance in her life. It's what she had dreamed of ever since she played house with Ken and Barbie. Barbie dying and leaving Ken a broken mess hadn't been part of the story. Her parents had the kind of love it seemed most people never found.

The kind you knew in your gut was going to stand the test of time. They were friends; they shared a sense of humor. After her mother's death, she watched her father fall to pieces. He never found love again. That nagging concern forced its way into every relationship Emma had, sometimes hammering away at her until she felt short of breath.

She had plenty of reasons to feel anxious at times. So far it hadn't grown to an overwhelming sort of "anxious," just a mildly frustrating, impatient anxiety that reared its head when she watched couples in love. It seemed they were everywhere: couples at the beach laughing, couples strolling in the park, couples walking their dog, couples at the playground enjoying their children. Men and women doing exactly what nature intended. Right behind every daydream of love came the fear losing it.

Emma sat in her office, staring at her computer screen. She read the same message for the sixth time, and still it didn't register. She pushed her chair back and spun around to look out across the ocean. It was times like this that she missed her mother the most.

"Accident, there has been an accident. I'm so sorry, your mother is gone." She rolled the word around on her tongue like she'd done so many times before. *Accident, accident.* It was a completely inadequate word to describe the devastating tragedy. It took years to shake the nightmares. She educated herself on death, the steps to heal. She knew in her heart you can never heal completely. Some days she just couldn't shake the thought that

maybe she had made a mistake in her career choice. Maybe she was a giant hypocrite. She wanted love in her life, until it was staring her in the face, which sent her running every time. Death had stolen her ability to love with any kind of freedom.

Her father remained a single man. He occasionally glanced at another woman, they occasionally spoke, but that was as far as it went. That was fine with Emma at the time because she couldn't imagine another woman trying to take her mother's place. Another woman wanting to move into their home, stealing their mother's place, was out of the question. She couldn't even imagine another woman kissing her father. With the passing of time, it seemed her father had given up on love. Maybe he thought the cost was just too high, or maybe he found it impossible to believe he would ever find that kind of love twice in a lifetime.

Crossing the room, she scooped up her bag with a change of clothes and crossed the hall to the ladies' room. She pulled her favorite old faded jeans from her bag and wiggled her behind into them. Standing with her back to the mirror, she twisted her head to see if they still held the desired effect. She knew without a doubt Brent was going to like what he saw. She caught him checking her out more than once. Starting any kind of relationship was unacceptable, but feeling desirable, even sexy, wasn't hurting anyone.

The bulky wool sweater irritated her skin, but she knew she would need it to keep warm from the icy fall wind. She never tired of watching the ocean showing off its powerful strength, tossing huge pieces of driftwood on the beach with ease. It helped put life's challenges into perspective.

***

Hope looked happy to see her as they strolled back down the driveway.

Emma reached for her backpack. "How about a walk on the beach?"

Hope took off running down the beach with her arms outstretched, pretending she was flying with the seagulls. Emma dropped the pack at the back door and took flight with Hope. Each step the stress of her day was dropping away behind her, left lying in the sand and being washed away beneath the waves. Seagulls squawked as they hung in the sky, enjoying the effortless flight. A bald eagle came in low behind her, falling and rising in the currents of air rushing across the sky and carrying him beyond the beach and out over the open water.

Emma stopped walking and found a log to sit on. She patted the spot beside her for Hope to sit.

"When I was a little girl, my mother and I used to sit and watch the eagles. We used to talk about all the places we would go if we could fly."

Hope sat close beside her for warmth, her hair flying wildly. "Where did you want to go?"

Emma sighed. "It was always different. Sometimes I didn't want to go anywhere. I just wanted to fly."

Hope leaned against her. "I would go to heaven and see my mom."

Emma brushed Hope's hair out of her eyes and

looked down at her. “Me too. I miss my mom.”

“Me too, Emma.”

Emma wrapped her arm around Hope’s shoulder. “I bet Heaven is pretty. I would stay for a while but I’d want to come back. I’d miss my dad and my sister too much to stay away.”

Hope looked into Emma’s eyes as she spoke. “I’d miss my dad too.” She stood and started walking back down the beach, dragging her shoe through the wet sand. “Daddy told me Mom is watching me from Heaven. What’s Heaven like?”

They continued down the beach.

Emma sighed. “I think Heaven is a wonderful place where we feel no pain or sadness. Your mother is watching over you, and I am absolutely certain she would want you to have the best life possible. She wants nothing more than your happiness. I bet she loves watching you smile and laugh.”

This was one of those moments that made her job satisfying. She remembered thinking the same things as Hope, and she also remembered being stuck in the sadness. She could not remember how long it took her to consider what her mother would have wanted for her. By the look on Hope’s face, the answers were what she was looking for. At least they appeared to bring her some peace.

Thunder rattled the sky. Emma looked up at the thick black clouds closing in on each other, squeezing out the first few drops of rain. She stood and offered her hand to Hope.

“We should get back to the house before nature decides to wash the beach.”

Hope stood and slipped her tiny warm hand into Emma's and squeezed. "I like you lots."

Emma smiled and squeezed her hand in return. "I like you lots too."

Another flash of light skipped through the black clouds, and close behind the thunder rolled. Not a moment later, the clouds burst open, flooding Hope and Emma with a heavy downpour. They locked hands and dashed for the house, laughing and squealing.

Brent stood holding the door open, waving the girls into the house. By the time they had reached the front door, they were dripping wet and leaving a puddle where they stood. Wrapping a towel around Hope, he sent her to find dry clothes.

Emma stood shivering in the doorway, her teeth chattering as she spoke. "I d-d-don't know why it n-n-never occurred to me to bring a ch-change of clothes."

He had already anticipated what she would need as he handed her his robe. "Why don't you go get the wet clothes off in the bathroom and hand them out to me so I can put them in the dryer? While you're in there, you may as well take a shower to get warm."

Heading toward the bathroom, she was grateful for the offer. "Thank you. Are you sure you d-d-d-don't mind?"

Brent laughed softly, apparently amused by her chattering teeth. He grabbed a towel from the hall closet and swung open the bathroom door.

One whole wall was a window, the view stretched from their secluded beach to the Coastal

Mountains out across the ocean. The antique-footed bathtub had more than enough room for two. Glass bottles filled with bath gels, bath salts, and thick lush towels rested on a restored antique table beside the tub. Add hot water, and your worries would vanish as your first toe sank beneath the bubbles. Tucked in close to it was a small round side table with a Tiffany lamp, women's reading glasses, and a romance novel with a pink beaded bookmark halfway through. Melissa's belongings sat there as if she were due back any day.

Brent's fingers skimmed across the cover of the book, marking a trail through the dust. He picked it up and carefully brushed the dust off before placing it back in the same place.

"I haven't removed any of her things yet. I'm not sure how to go about it." He paused for a moment, looking deep in thought. "Actually, that's not true. I like her things here." He turned and stepped out the door. "Hand me your wet things, and I'll throw them in the dryer."

It took Emma a few minutes to fight her way out of her wet clothes before opening the door a crack to hand them out to Brent. Her bra and panties were only damp and far too personal to add to the pile. She tugged the knob, starting a gentle fall of water from the overhead shower. She stepped inside and held her hand beneath the falling water. Steam rose from the tile floor. The hot water skimmed over her flesh, wrapping her in warmth. She closed her eyes and tilted her head back. Her toes stung and tingled as they warmed.

She stepped out of the shower and dried off.

Brent's robe hung from her like a small child in her father's overcoat. She fingered the fluffy pink robe hanging on the back of the door. She couldn't remember how long her mother's robe had hung on the back of their bathroom door; it seemed like years. No one ever mentioned it, and then one day it was gone.

***

Brent nudged Emma with his arm as he passed on his way to the fridge. "I'm glad you're staying for dinner, Emma. Not that you had much choice. I suppose you could have driven home in my bathrobe."

"I could have, but then I'd be missing this delicious feast and risk being spotted driving around town in a man's bathrobe. I can only imagine the stories that would have come out of that one." She winked at Hope. "Your neighbors would think I was a little nutty."

Hope piped up from the table. "Can I wear my robe and come with you?"

Brent smiled at Hope. "I guess if you're both going, I should come to. Wouldn't want the neighbors to think everyone in this house is crazy but me. Can we eat? Because dinner is ready."

He pulled a chair out for Emma and waited for her to sit and rested his hands on her shoulders, pausing. Every time he touched her, every damn time her breath caught in her throat. The man was thoughtful, kind, gentle, and so damned sexy.

The buzzer signaled to let them know the dryer

had finished. Emma squatted ever so carefully so as not to expose herself and scooped the ball of clothes from the dryer before heading to the bathroom to get dressed. She stepped into her still-warm jeans and sighed from the warmth on her skin. She was shocked to see her sweater had shrunk to less than half its original size. Tugging and wiggling, she managed to cover her breasts. She left the bathroom with her midriff completely exposed.

As Emma entered the living room, she struggled to keep from laughing. Brent's eyebrows shot up as he leaned back into the couch, grinning. Hope sat beside her father, unable to contain the laughter.

"I'm glad to see you both find this funny! Now, how about the two of you give me a hand?"

Brent slapped his hand to his chest. "I'm sorry. What can we do to help?" A grin spread across his face as his eyes roamed over her, drinking in the sight of her bare flesh. The taut skin across her flat belly still held remnants of her summer tan.

Hope covered her mouth, but giggles escaped through her fingers as she rolled off the couch and landed at Brent's feet.

Emma tried her best to keep a straight face as she spoke. "Maybe if Hope took a sleeve and pulled really hard, it would stretch."

The sweater wasn't going to stretch back into its original shape, but the game of trying sounded fun. Hope leaped to her feet and wrestled with a sleeve, making absolutely no headway but giggling hysterically. She pulled surprisingly harder than Emma expected. Emma shifted her weight into pulling in the opposite direction so Hope wouldn't pull her over.

Hope hung on as long as she could, but the sweater slipped from her fingers, sending Emma tumbling backward onto Brent's lap. His hands wrapped around her waist to soften her fall.

Emma scrambled off his lap, still laughing. "I'm sorry." The touch of his hands on her bare skin had sent a wave of goose bumps across her flesh.

Brent stood, continuing to keep his warm hand pressed to her lower back. "I'm the one that's sorry. Is this my fault? Was it the dryer that ruined your sweater?"

Emma tugged at the bottom of her sweater. "I think, um…a bit of, um…both. The rain…the rain…didn't help, either."

He moved his hands and rested them on her shoulders. "Would one of my t-shirts do for now? I promise I won't do any more of your laundry from now on."

She nodded in acceptance then found her sensible voice as soon as his hand left her. "That would be great, if you don't mind."

"Of course not. It's the least I could do. I'll be right back."

Back into the bathroom once more, Emma found herself inhaling deeply as she pulled the shirt over her head. It was far too big, and she tucked it into her jeans. The shoulder seams fell halfway down her arm. The countless times she gorged on romance novels, picturing the perfect male, had all come together in the doctor on the other side of the door. She leaned against the bathroom counter and rubbed the sleeve of the t-shirt, pressing it against her skin. The grin tugged at her cheeks. The attraction had taken on a life of its own.

Chapter Five

Love is wonderful, torturous, exciting, exhausting, exhilarating and heartbreaking. We all want that kind of love.

A month had passed in the blink of an eye, with every spare moment spent at the beach house. She met Hope at the bus stop, and they enjoyed the beach regardless of the weather. It was the hot spot for the best conversations. The sandy beach and fresh ocean air held a special charm. It was as if the wide-open space made even the scariest feelings and thoughts seem small.

They were on the right path, moving closer to a lighter heart with each passing day. According to Brent, he hadn't seen Hope smile in the last six months as much as she had in the last two weeks.

The evenings were much the same routine, which was best for Hope. Quiet meals with the three of them, light conversations, a walk on the beach—weather permitting—and finally a bubble bath for

Hope. It was in no way the routine for Emma. She had never devoted as much time to any one child; she had become entangled. It had become so much more than work.

Once Hope was off to bed, a few hours of relaxing in front of the fire with Brent took up the rest of the evening. Emma was enjoying the family experience a great deal, maybe too much. It wasn't her family. She was only here until Hope was feeling better. To be honest, it wasn't far off.

Hope trotted across the room dressed in her fuzzy warm pajamas covered in little brown teddy bears. "Good night, Emma."

Emma stood and gave Hope a quick hug. "I will be at the bus stop waiting for you tomorrow."

Hope backed up across the room. "Promise?"

Emma held up her left hand and placed her right hand across her heart. "Promise."

Hope turned on her heels toward her bedroom, calling behind her. "Come on, Dad."

Brent paused before following. "Can you stay awhile?"

He asked every night, and she stayed every night. It seemed she couldn't say no. Nothing inappropriate was going on, even though he now filled her thoughts day and night. The idea of falling into a sensual embrace, feeling his warm breath tickling her ear, kissing until the heat of arousal consumed every inch of her skin. He was fueling her fantasies, but fantasies they would have to stay. Fantasy was another word she was growing tired of. She was tired of fantasizing about the great romance she would never have.

Mike and Amy had finally gotten it right. They had found the man she had been waiting for, dreaming of. But it would mean breaking her number one rule. She did not, and would not ever, become romantically involved with anyone she was counseling, or the parents. Even if she considered waiting, for not only Hope but for Brent, it could take years. He showed signs of moving in that direction, but they were only glimpses. She had to wonder whether or not he was capable of falling in love with such intensity ever again. Whether or not he had a whole heart to give made all the difference. The fact remained, no one chose what their heart wanted, and Brent's heart was still full of love for Melissa.

Emma smiled and moved toward the loveseat. "I would love to stay. Take your time getting Hope tucked in."

As Brent moved down the hall, she dropped to the loveseat, crossed her legs, and stared out at the starry sky. The house was made for romance. Add Dr. Brent Forester and just like that, you had a perfect life. It was a shame it couldn't be her life. It was Melissa's. She was gone, but the house was still filled with her things, her memories, her daughter, and her loving, loyal husband. She could hear his footsteps as he returned. She licked her lips, adjusted her shirt, and fluffed her hair. Her heart fluttered once or twice—damn heart with a mind of its own.

Brent put another log on the fire in silence. He leaned against the mantle with one hand, staring into the flames licking at the bark. He seemed miles away and deep in thought about something.

"Is Hope all right?"

Brent looked confused. "Yes, yes, she was almost asleep before I left her room."

"Can I ask what has your thoughts miles away?"

"I was thinking about you. I was thinking I'd like to know more about you. I've taken up all of your time for the last month, and I don't know why it never occurred to me you must have a boyfriend. A woman as beautiful, intelligent, and kind must have men falling at her feet."

She watched his face closely, not wanting to miss his reaction.

"Nope. I'm kind of burnt out on the dating scene. I've decided to take a break now." She wasn't positive, but it looked like he felt relieved to hear she was single. "If you don't mind my asking, I'd like to know how you knew Melissa was *'the one'*?"

Brent glanced at her then turned his eyes back toward the fire. "Melissa was special. I knew the moment I saw her, I wanted her. We fit together perfectly, like we were made just for each other. I couldn't see her enough, couldn't touch her enough. I wanted to know everything about her. I wanted to share everything with her. I knew for certain it would last a lifetime." He patted his chest near his heart. "In here, I knew it in here. I never expected her life would be so short."

Emma moved beside him and sat by the fire. "I'm sorry she's gone."

Brent's thigh rested against hers. "It wasn't supposed to end like this. We had a plan; we were going to grow old together, enjoy our grandchildren, travel."

"At least you found it once, had real and true love. Not everyone is so lucky. It's not that I haven't given love a chance, I seem to have a hard time finding love at all."

Brent opened his hands and stared into his palms. "I find that hard to believe."

Emma continued to watch his expression, wishing she could read his mind. She couldn't seem to get a clear read on Brent, a clear picture of where he was in the grieving process. It wasn't like her, but neither was the overwhelming attraction. It was fogging her ability.

She tucked her hair behind her ear. "I've been in 'like,' came close to thinking maybe it could be love, but never have I found *that kind of love*." The comment sounded legitimate, but she knew it was a lie. She didn't trust love. It brought pain—the worst kind. She was looking it in the eye right at that very moment. Brent's pain was still there on his sleeve.

His gaze roamed over her face. "You are a beautiful, intelligent, interesting woman. The more time I spend with you, the more I find myself drawn to you. I'm certain there are plenty of men eager to have you in their lives."

At the mention of being drawn to her, she tilted her head slightly and batted her eyelashes. Her heart swelled, full of want and wish. It felt like it may burst if she didn't share it soon. This kind of behavior was completely out of character for her. She had been acting differently since their first meeting, feeling different, thinking different.

"There have been men. I wouldn't say plenty. It never felt right. I'm sure when I find him, *that* guy, *the* guy, I'll know it, just like you said. I want butterflies when I see him walk toward me. I want fireworks when we kiss. I want to smile every time I hear his name. I want it all and then some, but most importantly, I want him to feel the same." She turned her eyes away, her cheeks flushed. "In case it isn't obvious, I want a romantic love story."

He took her hand and helped her to her feet. "You deserve no less, Emma. How about we move to the sofa?"

He settled back into the seat. "Talk to me. Tell me about your life."

She smiled sheepishly. "What do you want to know?"

"Anything you want to tell me."

She started with her family, which of course led to her mother and the day of the accident. She locked her fingers together and tucked her hands under her chin.

"I was upset that day. This boy I really liked, he made fun of me in front of everyone. My mother was good at putting things into perspective, making things hurt a little less. I needed my mother and came in the back door to find my dad sitting at the kitchen table, looking at me through tears. My dad didn't cry, ever, so it terrified me. I felt my guts drop. I knew what he was going to say would be horrible. He told me to sit down beside him, but I wanted to run as far and as fast as I could. He said there was an accident, and after that, I only caught bits. It was my mom, and she was gone. I wanted to hide from the ugly words spilling out of him between sobs.

"You don't know how much I hate the word accident. It wasn't an accident. An accident is something that happens when people don't think. It was a drunk driver, an older man, with a family too. He knew he shouldn't be driving, but he did, and my family paid the price. He walked away with only a few scratches on his face. I know the inside scars will probably haunt him forever; I hope. How could they not?"

Without saying a word, Brent moved his hand across his lap and rested it on her forearm. He dropped his foot to the ground and moved in closer, his thigh warming hers.

She took a deep breath and let it out slowly. "My mother was my rock, my confidante, my friend, my keeper of secrets, my biggest fan. She was everything to me. I would have given anything to bring her back."

Brent listened intently, only nodding his head occasionally and handing her a tissue.

Emma dabbed at the corners of her eyes. "I'm sorry, I don't know why I'm crying. It's been years. You would think by now I could talk about her and not get all weepy."

He took her hand in his and cradled it gently. "No need to apologize, I'm here when you need to talk. You've been here for us. It's the least I can do. It seems to me the pain goes together with guilt."

Emma looked into his gentle, caring eyes. "Guilt? I don't understand."

Brent pulled his hand away. It turned to a fist,

and he buried it inside the other hand. His brow furrowed hard, forcing a small vein on the side of his forehead to push against the thin skin.

"It's ironic, really, all those years of school preparing myself to heal the sick, years of practicing medicine, and when I needed it most, I couldn't do a damn thing for the woman I loved more than life. I can't help but wonder if I missed something, if I helped her make the right treatment choices." Brent leaned forward and dropped his head in his hands.

Emma tenderly placed her hand on his back. "From what you've told me, Melissa was an intelligent woman, a strong woman. I find it difficult to believe she wouldn't play a large role in choosing her treatment. I also find it hard to believe you didn't spend every waking moment desperately searching for answers."

Brent raked his fingers through his hair. "I would have traded my life for hers."

Emma brushed her hand back and forth across his back. "If only."

Brent slouched down into the sofa and settled in. His broad shoulder rested against her. "I'm glad you're here. You sticking around for the evenings means a lot to me. I'm sure you have plenty of other things to do."

Emma shrugged her shoulders. "No actually, I don't. I enjoy my time here."

Brent's bare arm pressed against her. He lifted his hand to gesture, and his bulging bicep captured her attention once again. The heat from his thigh oozed through her jeans, and the butterflies were back torturing her once again. The thoughts crept back in, of kissing his lips, dragging a finger over the stubble covering his jaw. Climbing to his lap and feeling his powerful arms pull her close. He continued to act like the damn perfect gentleman he was.

Emma looked at her watch, surprised to see it was already going on midnight. Her emotions were getting the best of her, draining the last few ounces of energy she had. She pressed her hands to her knees and pushed herself off the couch with a groan. “I really should get going.”

Brent stood. “Of course, I didn’t mean to keep you so late. I’ll walk you out. Just let me get the flashlight.”

By the time he had returned, she was standing by the door waiting.

Brent leaned toward her, his face inches away. Emma shot her hand up to block him and pressed into his chest, stopping him dead in his tracks. In that split second, her common sense had leaped to the forefront. She had no idea how or why, but she was certain she was going to kick herself later.

“Excuse me.”

“Of course, where are my manners? If you will excuse me, I’ll get the door for you.” He reached around her and opened the door.

Emma’s face burned. “Oh…of course…the door.”

He had no intention of kissing her. He didn’t embarrass her any further than she already was by poking fun at her. She was certain he must think she was full of herself. They stepped outside, the cool air taking the heat off her cheeks.

Brent took her elbow for the walk across the yard and opened her car door. “So, I guess we will see you tomorrow then?”

Sliding down into her car, she smiled up at him. “Yes, of course, same time. I’ll be here to meet Hope when she gets off the bus.”

“Come whenever you want. The door is never locked. Whatever you want to do, it’s up to you.”

“That sounds good. Maybe I’ll come a little earlier in the afternoon and enjoy some quiet time on the beach…if you don’t mind, of course.”

He smiled and nodded. “Make yourself at home, beautiful. I’ll look forward to seeing you tomorrow.” Swinging her car door closed, he stepped back to watch as she drove away.

She knew Brent had interest in her, but she had no idea what he had in mind. She wasn’t about to start a conversation about the issue. All those years ago, she had tucked her heart away nice and safe, but it was cracking open for Brent and Hope. She had to wonder if the connection was a result of what had happened in her past. At times, watching Hope, it felt like she had gone to the side window, watching her own life unfold. She wanted nothing more than to help Hope find a way to keep her heart open, to heal and welcome all the love to come.

Chapter Six

You can want love, give love, feel love but you can't force love.

She knew things had crossed the line, she knew it when it was happening, but the word "no" seemed to have escaped her vocabulary.

Hope chatted excitedly about her day all the way to the mall. Her favorite store was a trendy younger women's shop, and she was anxious to try on everything. Emma settled into one of the seats near the change rooms and relaxed, while Hope strolled in and out with a new outfit every couple of minutes.

Pink hoodie, pink jeans, and pink running shoes stood before her. "You're making me crave cotton candy," Emma said.

Hope giggled. "Don't you just love pink?" Her eyes locked on a woman just a few yards away, and she took a step back. The smile quickly faded.

Emma reached out and touched her arm. "What's

wrong, Hope?"

"Do you ever think you see your mom? I know she's in Heaven, but sometimes I think I see her."

"I think we see people who look similar from behind or from the side. I think sometimes we see people who walk like them or have similar hair, and it reminds us of them. And I think we wish with all our hearts it is them."

Hope sniffled. "Were you mad at your mom for dying?" Her forehead scrunched up.

"Yes, I guess I was for a while. I mean I know the accident wasn't her fault, but if she hadn't gone out that day, or if she had driven a different route, she would still be here."

Hope wiped the tears from her eyes with the back of her hand and looked at Emma. "It's not fair. Why did it have to happen to my mom?"

She moved beside Hope and wrapped her arms around her. "I don't know why bad things happen sometimes. They just do. I remember the hurt came in waves. It would wash over me, and it was cold and hard to breathe. Then it would roll back out. The waves came frequently at first. They were big and rough and scary. After a while, they came less and less often, less scary."

Hope buried her face in Emma's shirt, wrapping her arms around her waist. "I hate when the waves come." A sob shook her delicate frame.

Emma stroked the silky curls. "I used to hate them too, but now, thinking back, each one took away little bits of pain. When I think of my mom now, the pain is so small compared to that first day." She took Hope by the shoulders. "I can tell you what helps me feel better sometimes. Instead of thinking about how unfair it is and how sad I am, I think about a time with my mom that was fun. Can you remember a time when you and your mother laughed?"

She looked at Emma with tear-stained cheeks. The corners of her mouth began to curl up as she spoke. "Mom and me used to go to the sunglass store and try them all on. We pretended we were movie stars and we needed the glasses for our disguise. We got in trouble once for getting fingerprints on all of them. Mom told them to be careful what they said because I was a famous movie star." Before Hope finished her story, she was laughing out loud.

Emma laughed with her and gave her a tender hug. "That's a wonderful story. Your mom was a funny lady. That's where you get it from."

Hope looked confused. "Where I got what from?"

Emma reached out and fingered one of Hope's blonde locks. "You got your sense of humor from your mom, just like your beautiful hair, the shape of your face, your gentle nature, your love for the beach, and so many other things. It is kind of like…a part of your mom is still alive inside you."

"What did your mom give you?"

Emma rested her hand on her heart. "My mom gave me so much, but most importantly she gave me lots and lots of love to share with everyone I meet. I like to think she is with me always, right here." Emma patted her chest. "I know your mom loved you more than anything else in the world, and she will always be in your heart."

Hope patted her own chest. "I like my mom being in here."

Emma sighed softly. "Me too, Hope, me too. Now shall we get back to our shopping?"

Hope perked up. "Can we go back to the hair holder place?"

Emma stood and picked up all the bags. "Sounds like a plan to me."

Hope was opening up to her more each day, talking, healing, and finding her happiness. Emma felt blessed to be a part of it. She felt blessed with every kid, but somehow Hope had wiggled her way a little further into her heart than the others ever had.

***

Pulling into the driveway, Emma was happy to see Brent's truck already sitting there. They entered the house calling his name, but there was no response. She sent Hope to get ready for the fashion show in the living room and stepped back outside to look for Brent. The banging around the side of the house had caught her ear, and she assumed it must have been Brent.

She rounded the corner of the house to catch Brent mid-swing. She quietly leaned her back against a tree and wrapped her arms across her chest for warmth. The ax hovered above his head for a second and came down with fierce speed, splitting the wood in half. Even with the chill of fall in the air, his white t-shirt, wet with sweat, clung to every flexed muscle across his broad shoulders and back.

He hadn't noticed her—and she had no intentions of changing that yet. As she watched his spectacular build do the rugged manliness of the chore, her thoughts turned to sexual fantasies. She bit her bottom lip and slowly ran her fingers through her hair, imagining it was his fingers. She dragged a finger down her neck and inside the collar of her shirt, touching where she ached for his lips to kiss. He raised the ax above his head and brought it down full force. With a thundering crack, the sharp steel forced its way through the wood, spreading it wide open. His biceps bulged and strained against the sleeve of his shirt. An involuntary moan slipping from her lips caught his attention.

Brent turned at the waist and wiped the sweat from his forehead with the back of his glove. His chest heaved with each breath. "Hi, Emma, glad to see the girls are home. Go on inside and get warm. I'll be in soon."

He had no idea how warm she already was. The cold fall air was no match for the heat flooding her skin. With a wave of her hand, she brushed her hair from her face. "Can I bring you anything?"

He gave her a warm smile. "No, but thank you."

She turned and started for the back door, listening for the steel to connect with wood once more, but it was quiet. She could feel his eyes watching her walk away and added a little extra wiggle. Pausing at the door, she tossed her hair over her shoulder and looked back, thrilled to see she was right. She hoped he enjoyed watching her.

A few moments later, Brent came in the back door packing an armload of wood. He passed Emma, smelling of wood and sweat, which was strangely arousing. He placed the pile by the fireplace and turned to face them.

"If you girls don't mind, I need a shower, and then I'm all yours."

Hope hugged her dad and then backed away, pinching her nose closed. "You smell awful."

Brent laughed and pulled her in for another hug. "Sorry, girls. I bet I do."

Emma stood close and picked a few wood chips from the sleeve of his t-shirt. "I don't know. I kind of like the smell of fresh-cut wood."

Hope backed away, still pinching her nose closed. "You should try hugging, Emma. It doesn't smell like wood."

Her cheeks burned as she stepped back. She wanted nothing more than to sink into his arms, press her lips to his. "I'll take your word for it, Hope."

Brent opened his arms and moved toward Hope. "I think Hope wants another hug."

Hope squealed her way down the hall toward her bedroom as Brent chased her. He must have caught her because the squealing had turned to laughter. Emma sank into the chair and smiled. Hope was doing well, better than she had expected. They weren't going to need her counseling services much longer and had yet to discuss what Brent wanted to do about finding a long-term housekeeper and nanny. She would be willing to help until they found a good fit. It was difficult for her. She was enjoying playing house, but if it went on much longer, the risk of Hope getting too attached was increasing. As much as she hated the idea of leaving them, it was inevitable.

Brent sauntered past her and into the laundry room. She stood and followed as far as the kitchen. He returned a moment later naked from the waist up. His jeans sat on his hips, exposing the band of his boxers and the smooth taut skin of his abdomen. He stood before her with the sexiest grin she had ever seen. A rush of heat raced for her cheeks again. She closed her mouth the second she realized it was hanging open.

Hope ran to Brent and hugged his waist. With pleading eyes, she looked up. "Emma said she would stay to play Monopoly if it was okay with you."

"I'm up for it if you are, but be assured I am the Monopoly champion."

Hope patted her father's bare chest. "Don't make me laugh."

Brent tickled Hope, sending her squealing back into the kitchen. "We'll just see who's laughing at the end of the game." He turned toward Emma. "I guess I'd better go hit the shower if I want the girls to sit near me."

Emma leaned against the kitchen counter. "Go ahead and shower. Hope and I will finish up dinner." She continued to stand there and stare.

Brent turned and headed back across the room. "Sounds great, girls. See you in a few minutes."

"Still shirtless, I hope," snuck out of her mouth. Emma quickly turned her face away.

Brent turned back. "Sorry, Emma, I didn't catch what you said."

She didn't look up as she answered, for fear he would read what was written all over her face. "Um…don't forget to use soap."

As ridiculous as it sounded, it was better than repeating what she said the first time. Noticing his chest was one thing; asking to see it for the rest of the evening was completely inappropriate. The fact the words popped out of her mouth was shocking enough; it wasn't like her. This man had her acting like a woman she didn't know. Flaunting her figure, blatantly flirting, and now verbalizing every little thought? What was next, physically throwing herself?

Everyone pulled an overstuffed pillow up to the coffee table and got comfortable. Hope rounded the Monopoly game, buying up every property and thoroughly enjoying bankrupting Emma and her father.

Emma's legs were cramping. She stretched them out in front of her to relieve the pain only to kick the table with her baby toe. She let out a whimpering giggle. "Nothing hurts like stubbing your toe."

Brent reached under the table and cradled her foot in his hands to rub it through the pain. "Let me know if I'm being too rough."

She smiled across the table. "Thank you, Doctor, definitely not too rough. In fact, I would say just right."

His large hand wrapped around her ankle, the other caressing the top of her foot and her toes, the tingling arousal working its way up her leg to the inside of her thigh.

Hope chimed in. "Daddy gives really good back rubs, too. Daddy, why don't you give Emma a back rub?"

Emma watched Brent's face flush as he quickly released her foot and lifted himself to his feet.

He turned Hope toward her bedroom and lovingly tapped her on the back. "Because I'm going to tuck you in bed instead. Now go brush those teeth and get in your pajamas."

Hope dragged her heels as she walked down the hall, muttering under her breath.

Brent reached a hand out and pulled Emma up. "Why don't you stretch your leg on the way to the kitchen and get us another glass of wine?" He continued to hold her hand once she was standing. "That is if you can walk on that toe. I'll go tuck Hope in and be right back."

"I would like to stay and talk, but I still have to drive home, and one glass of wine is my limit."

"Then spend the night and help me finish the bottle. The spare room is ready and waiting. You know it wouldn't hurt to have a few things here, an overnight bag, just for occasions like this."

The voice inside her head screamed, "No," yet the exact opposite slipped from her lips. Excuses tumbled like dominos. It was Friday, she didn't have to work, it was cold outside, and it definitely sounded a lot better than going home and being alone.

She tilted her head to one side. "If you're sure? It sounds like a great plan to me."

He leaned close to her cheek and whispered, "I'm sure. Meet me back here in a few minutes."

She sat on the loveseat, wine glasses filled. She had a few moments to convince her mind she wasn't making a big mistake, a few moments to mull over the latest event. Maybe it wasn't that bad of an idea; maybe it could work. The way he grinned at her, the way he touched her tenderly, caressing her ankle, it meant something. Her gut instincts were telling her he felt something. It was a little confusing at times, but something.

When he returned, instead of sitting beside her on the loveseat, he chose to sit across the room from her, and the confusion leapt to the forefront once again. It felt like being on the merry-go-round, hop on, hop off.

Emma broke the silence. "Hope is an amazing girl. She has made some real progress these past few weeks. Considering what she's been through in the last year, she's doing very well."

Brent took a deep breath and released it slowly. "Hope is everything to me. If not for her, I would have gone into hiding. I think she's doing pretty well now, thanks to you. We have our moments when things get rough, but for the most part, we're good. My work can get demanding at times, and that's not about to change, but thankfully that's where you come in."

Emma ran her fingers through her hair. "I'm glad I'm here." She finished the last of her wine, maybe a little too quickly, and set the glass on the table in front of her. "I think you're doing an amazing job with Hope. It can't be easy. I experienced Hope's side of it. I mean, I watched my father, but I don't really know what it was like. I don't really know what it's like for you, but I'm all ears if you want to talk."

Brent continued to poke at the fire. "That's why I think we got lucky finding you. You know better than most what Hope is going through."

Emma gave an opening to discuss where he stood, but it was very clear he wasn't willing just yet. She was hoping to get a little insight on where he was on his journey back. How far had he made it in the healing process? Was he ready to start a relationship, ready to date, ready for her? She had so many questions and all of them none of her business. She had no right to ask. Brent had requested her help for Hope, not himself.

She fussed with her sleeve. "It's nice to know you consider yourselves lucky. I have to admit I look forward to coming here all day, which brings me to something we should discuss."

"What's that, Emma?"

She swung her feet to the floor and leaned forward, resting her elbows on her knees. "Hope isn't going to need me soon. I don't know what your plans are for afterward. I kind of assumed you might still be looking for a nanny."

Brent turned to look at her with concern. "Please tell me we still have you for a while."

Emma shrugged her shoulders. "For a short while, I'm afraid. I will always be available for Hope to talk to if she needs me. I do think it would be best for you to find a nanny as soon as possible. Would you like me to look into it for you?"

Brent furrowed his brow. “I’m sorry. I assumed…I mean, I thought you would be around longer.”

“Please don’t think I don’t love coming here. I do, but Hope is not going to need me at all one day. I think it would be best if she didn’t have the chance to get overly attached. I would be more than happy to help you find the nanny best suited for her. I’m involved until she adjusts.”

“If you think that’s best.” He rose and moved back to the fireplace and poked at the embers.

She clasped her hands together in her lap. “It doesn’t have to end right away. We have a few weeks.”

Brent crossed the room. “A few weeks it is.” He offered his hand to her. “I’m going to miss your company at night. It’s lonely here after Hope goes to bed.” He swallowed the last mouthful of wine and placed the glass on the table. “We should get some sleep.”

The conversation had gone somewhere he wasn’t interested in discussing. A few moments before, he had wanted to spend the evening talking and relaxing, but now it was as if he was eager to get her to her bed and be alone.

She smiled and took his hand. “I enjoy our evenings as well. I’m sure I’ll miss them also.”

He continued to hold her hand as they moved down the hall in silence toward the spare room. Leaning against the wall outside her room, he caressed the back of her hand as he spoke. “Thank you for being so great with Hope, and thank you for everything you do around here. I know it’s only been a short time, but we will miss you."

She placed her hand on his chest, feeling the warmth of his body through his shirt. The touch held so much unspoken meaning, and she wished he could read her thoughts. She wondered if he could feel it, how she ached to drag Brent into her room and make love for the rest of the night.

Emma shrugged her shoulders. "I'm not going anywhere tonight, just to sleep, so I will see you in the morning."

She stripped down and crawled into bed. Alone with her thoughts, it felt wrong, all of it. He was lonely; he had lost the love of his life. He was probably just filling the empty nights with the company. Anyone would. He had discussed Hope's needs, what he wanted for her, finding her happiness. He was a devoted, reliable, responsible, loving father. Who wouldn't want that in a man?

Melissa had been gone close to a year, and he was struggling with removing her personal things, things that would bring her to mind more often. He struggled with relaxing and just having fun, like it wasn't something he allowed himself to do. Whether he was unaware or in denial, he needed to start letting some things go himself to move forward. Just because he was a doctor didn't mean he was expected to face the death of his wife alone.

Her father was a proud strong man, and it broke Emma's heart watching him struggle, suffering alone. He never found another woman, and she had no right to push for it. Maybe he knew there would never be another woman he loved like his wife, and maybe he was right. Maybe Brent had made the same decision.

Chapter Seven

Turns out death isn't the only way to make you suffer.

A knock at the bedroom door forced Emma to pry open her red swollen eyes. She had spent the night, and it was a bad idea. She was struggling with her own demons, and they had brought on a bout of tears before she fell asleep.

Brent's scratchy morning voice eased through the closed door. "Emma, are you up?"

She had to clear her throat before replying. "Yes, thank you. I will be out in a few minutes."

"Take your time. The bathroom is all yours if you want to shower. I left you some towels."

She heard his footsteps fade down the hall. She rubbed her itchy burning eyes. It was all so ridiculous, mourning something she never truly had.

By the time she had dressed and made a quick pit stop in the washroom, Brent had breakfast already going. Hope was up, dressed, and head-first in the fridge looking for the juice. She poured everyone a glass and put them on the table. She pulled out three plates, three forks, and three napkins, then arranged them on the table.

Emma stood near the entrance to the kitchen. "You have this breakfast thing down. You're very lucky to have such a helpful young assistant."

Brent looked up from the frying pan but continued to stir the eggs. "You bet I am. I couldn't do it without her."

Hope sat down. "You can sit by me, Emma. Dad makes really good scrambled eggs. He puts cheese in them."

Emma eased herself to the chair. "Thank you, Hope. The eggs do smell wonderful."

Brent divided up the eggs and sat on the other side of Emma. "I assume you're still planning on spending the day."

"Yes, of course. I promised Hope, and I always keep my promises."

"The hospital called me. I have to go in for a few hours. Will you two lovely women be okay until I get back?"

Emma never looked up from the table. "We'll be fine."

Brent had barely spoken to her through breakfast, and he had pulled back from her when she stepped closer to him. He was still smiling and continued with the polite conversation, but something had changed. It felt as though he had already said good-bye.

Hope stood and started tugging her toward the hall. "Can you please do my hair?"

She paused beside Brent. “We need to talk.”

Brent avoided her stare. “Of course, later today.”

Emma called back over her shoulder as she followed Hope down the hall. “Fine.”

She had no intentions of changing anything with Hope, but her evenings were spent at home from now on. Problem solved, only a few moments of interaction with Brent Monday to Friday; she couldn’t manage any more.

Emma picked up the dirty plates and piled them in the sink. “Let’s leave the dishes and go for a little hike. I know a beautiful place.”

A quick stop at home to change and they were on their way to the park. Due to cougar sightings in the park and the odd dog getting a little too aggressive, she had taken up cupping pepper spray in her hand. Better safe than sorry, her mother always said. She hadn’t exactly been following that simple rule with Brent.

It was brisk outside, and the cool air brought some life into her body. Squinting from the sunlight sparkling off the ocean, she scanned the park for other hikers. She preferred some traffic. Safety in numbers took on a whole new meaning when she hit the trails that ran through the woods. The trail was empty—an unusual thing, especially on such a beautiful morning.

The trail narrowed as they entered the woods. Something inside her said to turn back, stick near the beach, but that would mean taking the long route home. The woods were only a few miles, and they would be out on the road in no time.

The sound of a twig snapping had her cranking

her neck around. Something was rustling through the bushes, moving in the same direction.

She gripped Hope's hand a little tighter. "Maybe we should walk a little faster. Is that okay? Can you move a little faster?"

Hope's fist tightened in return. "Is something wrong, Emma?"

Emma cranked her head around again, scanning the woods, all her senses on high alert. She turned and picked up the pace, straining her ears for any sound. Nothing, it was probably nothing. She hated when her overactive imagination had any sort of control. She was scaring Hope.

"No, honey, I just wanted to keep warm, and it helps to move a little faster."

She glanced over her shoulder. The sun made it hard to see. Yet even with a quick glance through squinted eyes, there was no mistaking it was a large animal. The figure looked a lot like a cat, moved like a cat. Fear was poking at her gut and tightening her chest. She white-knuckled the pepper spray with her index finger poised over the nozzle, ready.

Her eyes darted back and forth, scanning the park looking for other people, anyone at all. They had another quarter-mile to go before she came to the road. She spun her head around for another look. Whatever it was, it was gone. Her eyes darted from one shadow to the next.

The animal had moved into the thick underbrush, close behind her, breaking the occasional branch. Her heart pounded in her chest, thundering in her ears.

She stumbled, her legs trying to catch up;

releasing Hope's hand, gravity won and dropped her to the ground, her fist still gripping the pepper spray. She scrambled to her feet.

Hope tugged at her hand. "Emma, hurry."

She gingerly took a step, then another. It was painful but doable. Emma knew Hope could sense the urgency, but she didn't want to scare her unnecessarily.

She took a few steps, and the pain shot up her leg. She had to get Hope out of the woods, out in the open. She took another step and winced, and another step. She had a plan. If the cougar came at them, she would put herself between them, get him close, and one good shot in the eye—giving Hope time to run.

Her ankle screamed at her with every step as they hurried along the trail. Forcing each step, blocking the want to whimper out of agony, she made her way toward the edge of the forest. Her protective instincts had kicked in, strong, overpowering every other thought. Her shoe had grown tight against her ankle. Tell-tale signs of a good sprain. The pain was going to worsen substantially as soon as the adrenaline wore off.

Hope did her best to help, focusing on Emma's pain, a furrowed brow exposing her concern. They finally stepped onto the sidewalk and released a heavy sigh in unison.

Emma pulled Hope close to her chest and kissed the top of her head. "We're okay. That was a little scary, but we're okay now."

Hope's arms wrapped around Emma's waist as she looked up at her. "I wasn't scared. I know you won't let me get hurt."

Emma cupped Hope's rosy little cheeks in her hands and kissed her forehead. "I would have fought that cat with my bare hands before I let it hurt you."

Hope smiled a toothy grin. "I know, because we're best friends and you love me."

Emma's heart swelled, and the threat of tears pinched her throat. She loved Hope. The sweet girl had worked her way into her heart regardless of how determined she was to stay focused on her reasons for being here. They taught her at school to keep her heart at a safe distance; getting too close, too involved, hindered her ability to see things clearly. She had broken an important rule of being a good counselor, and it made no sense because her job meant everything to her.

She rested her hands on Hope's shoulders and spun her around to face the car. "Let's go home, friend."

***

Pulling into the driveway, Emma half expected to see Brent's truck. She checked her watch. It was still early in the afternoon. Worn out from the excitement and the brisk hike, Hope was settled in watching a movie. There was plenty of time for a hot bath to take the chill off and soak her sore ankle.

She filled the tub and slipped out of her hiking gear. She eased into the hot water and settled back to watch time peacefully pass by. She soaked until the water was lukewarm.

Stepping out of the tub, she turned to check the cabinet for towels, and their eyes met. Her heart pounded like a drum, ringing in her ears. Her cheeks were on fire. She had no idea how long Brent had stood there, but from the look on his face, he was just as surprised to see her. A small hand towel was the only thing available, and she scrambled to cover herself, an impossible task. When she looked up again, he was gone.

She dried off as quickly as she could with the tiny towel, regretting not checking for a bath towel before she climbed into the tub. Still a little wet, she forced her way into her jeans and pulled her t-shirt over her head. In her rushed state, she forgot to put her bra back on, and there was no way the shirt was coming back off. Not now, anyway.

She moved over to the mirror, shoved her bra into the pocket of her jeans, and groaned at her reflection. She hobbled to the door and held the knob in her hand, summoned all her nerve, and turned the doorknob.

Brent was poised to knock on the door, and they startled each other when the door opened, and they found themselves face to face.

His eyes locked on hers. "I was just coming to see if you were okay."

She covered her eyes with her hand. "I'm fine. I mean, what happened is okay. I mean, I'm okay."

Brent shoved his hands in his pockets. "Oh, okay. That's good. You shouldn't be embarrassed."

"Well, I am, but I'm sure I'll get over it. It was my fault. I should have closed the blinds."

"With a body like that, I can't imagine why you

would be embarrassed." He started to back away and then turned back, looking down at her shirt. "You look cold." He unzipped his sweatshirt, took it off, and wrapped it around her shoulders.

As he turned to leave, he spotted her little black G-string underwear on the vanity and lifted them with his index finger. He took her hand in his and turned it over, dangling the panties inches from her palm. "You want these, or can I keep them for a memento?"

Emma snatched them from his finger. "I'm so glad you find this so or amusing." She winced in pain.

Brent furrowed his brow. "You all right?"

"I will be. I twisted my ankle on our walk this afternoon."

She stepped out the door, her panties still in her hand. With nowhere else to put them, she shoved them in the front pocket of his sweatshirt.

Hope hopped up and down beside her dad. "It was kinda scary but kinda fun, Daddy. We went for a walk in Emma's favorite place, and we almost got eaten by a cat. It followed us in the bushes. Emma was brave. She had spray stuff to make it go away." She paused and looked at Emma. "What did you call it? Tell Daddy what you called it."

Brent frowned and hugged Hope to his chest. "Can you please go set the table for lunch?"

He waited a moment for Hope to get out of earshot. "How could you put Hope in danger? The cougar warning notices are up everywhere, Emma." His voice was gruff while trying to keep it down so Hope wouldn't hear. "You were hired to do a job;

what the hell happened?" He raked his fingers through his hair, pacing back and forth. "Who do you think you are, Emma? I thought I could trust you to keep her safe." He put his hand up to silence her. "You are not her mother. I don't need you running her all over the place. She's all I have left, for Christ's sake." The scowl deepened, and he shook his head. "I trusted you. Clearly, that was a mistake."

Emma's eyes stung. "I'm sorry. You are absolutely right. I shouldn't be here. It's the weekend, and this is all very inappropriate." She moved to the door, fighting the tears straining to get out. "My keys, my purse…" She frantically scanned the room, blinking to clear her vision. "I'm sorry. I'm so sorry, Brent."

She shoved one foot into her runner and headed out the door carrying the other—her ankle wasn't going to tolerate anything else.

Brent stood watching her, the scowl still firmly in place. "Put your other shoe on."

She gripped the handrail and limped down the few steps, not looking back. "I can't. My ankle is swollen." Hot tears poured down her cheeks. She kept moving as he continued to call after her.

"Wait a minute, let me get my shoes," he hollered after her.

Jogging and hopping, and wincing with every step, she couldn't stop moving. A few more feet and she would be in her car, alone, and she could let everything go.

Brent was right. What had happened in the last few months was so much more than she should have allowed. Tears blurred her sight as she slammed the car door shut. She ground them out of her way to start the car. This was the pain she had run from. It didn't take a death to crush her, just her own stupid lack of control. It was time to remove herself. It was going to take every ounce of strength she could muster to remain professional and composed.

Chapter Eight

Real and true love means doing what's right, what's best for the ones you love, even when it means falling to pieces yourself.

Emma sat in her office, a beautiful young woman in her mid-twenties across from her.

Four years of experience caring for a family in England, one child with special needs, and a long list of credentials and references put her miles above all the other applicants. She was an incredible find, and they would have to act fast or they would lose her to another family.

Emma sat staring at her, wishing she wasn't so attractive, so sweet, and so single. Older women had applied for the job of the nanny, but she appeared to be the fullest of life, energy, and had a great spirit. She would do wonders for Hope, and that was what sealed the deal.

"I'll need to call your references, and of course the young girl's father will need to meet with you."

A soft, sweet, confident voice answered her. "Of course, ma'am. I understand."

Emma cringed. "Please don't call me ma'am. It's Emma. I'm not that much older than you."

"Of course, ma'am. Sorry…Emma."

Emma pushed her chair back and leaned over her desk to shake her hand. "I'll let you know as soon as I have a time and place to meet with them. Thank you for coming in."

"Thank you, ma'am, I mean Emma."

The door clicked behind her as Emma leaned back in her chair and picked up the phone. No point in prolonging the inevitable. As it was, she would still be around for a few more weeks. The last thing she needed was more time to consider why Brent didn't, couldn't, or wouldn't let things move forward.

Brent answered on the third ring. "Hello."

"Hello, Brent, it's Emma."

"Good to hear your voice."

"I have some good news. I found your nanny." There was background noise, but Brent had fallen silent. "Hello, are you still there?"

Brent cleared his throat. "I'm here." He paused. "So, you found us a nanny?"

"Yes, I think I've found the perfect fit. I'd like you to meet with her as soon as possible or we could risk losing her."

He grumbled as he spoke. "Wouldn't want to do that."

Emma tried to keep the emotion out of her voice. "Is something wrong? Did I catch you at a bad time?"

"No, of course not. It's just that…I mean, I thought…you said we had a few weeks."

"And we still do. I would never leave Hope without giving her time to adjust."

"It may take longer than a few weeks."

Emma sighed. "It may, but I doubt it. You're going to like this girl. I'm sure of it."

"Hmmm, I'll take your word for it."

"So, when would you like to meet her?" He sounded annoyed when he had no right. She was doing exactly what she said she would. He could have given her a reason to hold off, he could have asked her to wait for him, but he didn't. She was only doing what made sense. Brent was not answering. "Are you still there?"

"Yes, I'm still here. I'm checking my schedule. It looks like the only time open is next Friday. How's that sound?"

"Next Friday, are you serious?" She tossed her pen onto her desk.

"Sorry, Emma, that's the best I can do. I'm a little busy now. Can we talk when I get home?"

Emma huffed. "I suppose I don't have much choice. I'll bring you the information on the nanny."

"Sounds great. Can you stay awhile and go over it with me? I'll pick up a bottle of your favorite wine. See you this evening."

The phone clicked in her ear before she could respond. She would stay only as long as it took to go over the information, and there would be no wine involved.

Emma dropped into the seat and adjusted the steering wheel. The folder sitting on the seat beside her had her guts in a tangled mess. It held all the information on the nanny. The woman would spend her days with Brent and Hope. She had no right to feel jealous, but she did. She had no right to feel hurt, but she did. She had no right to feel like the nanny was taking them away, because they were never hers.

The bubbly, beautiful young nanny would be living at the beach house sharing her life with Brent and Hope. She would be caring for them, walking the beach, laughing, talking, and being everything. Everything Emma had ever wanted and more. Emma knew in her heart she belonged with Brent and Hope—they would have been great together. It was that kind of love, and she knew it with more certainty than she had ever felt in her life.

Tears rolled down her cheeks, and she brushed them away with the back of her hand. There was no point in dragging it out any longer than necessary; her heart couldn't take it. She would push for an earlier introduction with the nanny and get things moving along. She sucked in a deep breath and let it out slowly. She had no business feeling sorry for herself.

Her chest felt like the weight of the world was resting on it. She dropped the folder on the kitchen counter and brushed her hand across the cold paper. She balled up her fist and slammed it on the folder, spun on her heels, and walked out the door.

The wind cut through her sweater like a knife as she walked down the driveway. Her skin hurt, her mind hurt, and her heart was beyond hurt.

Hope bounced off the bus, giggling, and ran to

Emma for a hug.

"Hi, Emma, guess what happened today."

Emma tucked away her sadness. It would have plenty of opportunities to crush her, suffocate her later that evening. She smiled down at Hope. "I can't even begin to imagine, so I think you're going to have to tell me."

Hope giggled again into her palm. "Brandon tried to kiss me on the lips."

Emma covered her mouth and giggled back. "Did you let him?"

Hope bounced up and down on the spot, still giggling, still covering her mouth as she spilled her fantastic secret. "I did. I kind of liked it, but it was kind of yucky, too. His lips are really wet and slippery." She giggled hysterically again.

Emma scooped her hand and started the walk back down the driveway. "What part did you kind of like?"

Hope skipped beside her, still holding her hand. "He tasted like peanut butter and jelly. I liked the peanut butter part, but I hate the sticky jelly."

"I know exactly what you mean. It's a shame some relationships have a sticky part." Hope had no idea what sticky parts she was referring to. She had created a sticky mess of her own with Brent. She had no idea how she was going to drag her heart away and manage to stay away. She shivered as the wind cut through her sweater once again.

Hope flung open the back door and dropped everything at the entrance. She turned to face Emma with a straight face. "It made my tummy feel funny, like when I eat a lot of candy. It was all bouncy inside."

Emma tucked a finger under her chin. "So you like this boy?"

She shrugged her shoulders and headed for the fridge, talking with her back turned to Emma. "Does it feel like that when Daddy kisses you?"

Emma froze to the spot. They hadn't kissed, so there was no kiss for Hope to see. She had always been careful around Hope, careful not to show any inappropriate behavior. She had kept it all friendly and safe on the outside.

Emma fumbled for words. "I…well…Hope…your daddy and I have never kissed. What would make you think we had, sweetheart?"

She continued to rummage through the fridge, looking for just the right snack. "Because you love each other." She stated it like it was no more than common knowledge.

Emma moved into the kitchen, carefully choosing her words. "Hope, I care about your father, he is a very special man, but I don't love him. We are not in love."

Hope looked up from the fridge and smiled. "Yes, you are, and I know because you act just like Mommy and Daddy used to."

Emma leaned against the kitchen counter and picked the folder up, the folder holding their future, the folder that would change everything. She placed it on top of the fridge out of sight.

She leaned into the fridge behind Hope and joined the search while gently informing her, "I'm sorry you got that impression, but your father and I don't love each other in that way."

When the two stood with pickles and cheese in hand, they stepped back and swung the fridge door closed. Emma saw him first standing at the door. Brent looked like someone had just punched him in the gut. He turned his back on them and shrugged off his jacket, hung it on the hook, and paused before turning to face them again.

Emma wanted to ask how long he had been standing there, how much of their conversation he had heard, if he wanted to correct her and tell Hope otherwise, but she didn't.

He opened his arms for a hug from his daughter, his eyes never leaving Emma's. "I broke away early today. I had a few things to take care of."

Emma stepped toward the fridge and pulled the folder down. "I brought something for you to look at. It's important that you read it tonight because I'd like to get going on it as soon as possible. In fact, I was thinking tomorrow."

Brent took the folder from her hand, brushing his fingers over the back of her hand. "What is it, Emma?"

Emma stepped past him, sucking in a deep breath and holding it tight, knowing only a few more times would she smell him, hear his voice, feel his touch. A sob almost broke free.

She couldn't turn to face him or all would be lost.

She spoke without looking back. "The folder is self-explanatory." She closed the door behind her and couldn't get to her car fast enough. A flood of tears was bursting to get out, and she refused to get caught by Brent or Hope.

The car jerked and moaned beneath her. She wasn't focusing on the task and almost drove into a tree. She slammed on the brakes at the end of the driveway, well out of their sight, and pounded her fist on the steering wheel. Every inch of her broken body ached. She felt drained of the joys of love and life. All she had to face her now was an empty, lonely life and a stack of romance novels sitting on her nightstand waiting for her to insert her name.

Chapter Nine

There is always room for more love.

Amy continued to pull items from the trunk and hand them to Emma. "This is a fabulous idea. I'm glad you called. We haven't had a picnic at the beach in ages."

"I'm glad you guys were up for it. I need a day of peace and family."

"Jessie is hardly peaceful." Amy laughed. "I don't feel like I've seen much of you this last while. Actually, it's been since you started working for Brent."

Emma shrugged her shoulders. "I know. I'm sorry. It's been a crazy time for me. Lots going on, but we have all day to catch up."

Amy shut the trunk and grabbed Emma by the elbow. "Let's hit the beach and you can start by telling me what you think of Brent. Are there sparks?"

Emma rolled her eyes. "Seriously, Amy, you and

your husband are going to drive me crazy."

Amy squeezed Emma's elbow. "Crazy is not what we had in mind, more like madly in love. If crazy is what it takes to get you there, so be it."

Emma leaned close to Amy and bumped her with her shoulder. "If it makes you feel better, there are sparks for me. I couldn't stop them if I wanted. As for Brent, I have no idea what he's thinking, and it doesn't matter because it would be wrong."

Amy rolled her eyes. "How on earth could it be wrong?"

Emma dropped her armload of stuff next to the picnic table and dragged her fingers through her hair. "I don't believe in getting romantically involved with the parents, Amy." She sat down with a thud onto the bench. "It wouldn't be right, and you know how I feel about the kids, about what I do."

Amy sat beside her and brushed Emma's hair over her shoulder. "You and your rules, Emma. I think just this once you should break one."

Emma sighed. "I've never felt anything like it before, in my heart, in my mind. I think he feels the same at times, then other times he's so distant."

Amy rubbed her shoulder. "You are the first after Melissa. He probably finds himself feeling confused or guilty."

Emma patted the back of Amy's hand still resting on her shoulder. "You're probably right, and that's the reason I have rules. Besides, as selfish as it sounds, I don't want some small corner of his heart. I don't want him to 'settle' after his one true love. I want wild, crazy, passionate love that's all mine."

Amy stood and crossed her sweater over her chest for warmth. "I think you should give it some time. Let him get used to the idea of letting go of Melissa and letting another woman into his heart. It's difficult, figuring out how to let go, knowing when your heart is ready to take a chance on love again."

"I would imagine it is, and I feel for him, truly I do. But I'm creeping up on thirty, and I don't feel like I have a lot of time to wait."

Amy rolled her eyes. "You make it sound like you're turning a hundred. You're twenty-eight and in fabulous shape. You have plenty of time. Besides, I don't think it will take that long for Brent to come around. It's almost been a year—he's certainly honored Melissa's memory. He stayed strong and did right by Hope. I would think because he hasn't gone chasing every skirt in town, that makes him worth waiting for." Amy gently tugged at one of Emma's curls hanging down her back. "You, my gorgeous sister, probably have him doing everything in his power to make the next move. He'd be crazy not to."

Emma smiled at Amy. "Thanks for the compliment. There are a lot of things that make him worth waiting for. Problem being, I'm waiting for something that's never going to happen. I have tried to open the door for a discussion, but he's not ready."

"Let's go for a walk." She hooked her hand in Emma's elbow and called back over her shoulder, "Mike, please keep both eyes on Jessie?" She squeezed her elbow. "I can hardly wait till you have one of your own. I bet Brent would make a handsome son."

Emma nudged her back. "I wish you would stop talking about it, because it's not going to happen."

Amy stopped walking. "Why couldn't it happen? Sometimes rules need to be broken."

"I didn't say it couldn't. I said the option was not available. Just to clear things up—this is my number one rule, Amy, and for good reason. I refuse to hinder their healing time in any way."

"Do you want me to get Mike to talk to him, find out where he stands?"

"No…oh, God no…please, just let things be. I mean it, Amy."

Amy stopped and put her hand on Emma's shoulder, turning her to face her. "Please don't be angry with me, but I think you're making excuses. I think every time you find yourself getting close to a man, you find a reason or something wrong, so you can make your escape."

Emma backed off and turned back toward the picnic table. "Don't be ridiculous. Why would I do such a thing?"

Amy almost had to jog to keep up with Emma's pace. "I don't know…afraid, I guess."

Emma stopped so abruptly Amy bumped into the back of her. Emma spun around and threw her hands up in the air. "What exactly would I be afraid of, Amy? Afraid of ending my loneliness? Afraid of being consumed with all the joy a family brings, afraid of loving a man so much I would rather die than face my life without him?" Emma cupped her hand over her mouth and stared at Amy. Tears stung the back of her eyes.

Amy gripped Emma's wrists. "Yes, I do. I mean, I understand completely. You were older than me, you knew more, and you watched Dad and you could see what it was like for him. All I can tell you is, it's worth the risk, Emma. You have to stop finding excuses to push them away. I want you to feel what I feel. I want you to have a love that makes you feel like a queen. Brent is that man; I can feel it. Please just tell me you will at least consider giving it a chance."

Emma pulled her hands free and brushed the tears from her cheeks. "I want to, Amy."

"I love you, you're my big sis, and you have always been there for me since Mom died." Amy pulled Emma in for a hug. "I love you, sis." She watched over Emma's shoulder as her father's car pulled up to the beach. He waved and then moved to the other side of his car, opened the door, and helped a woman out. "Oh, my…Emma! I don't believe my eyes."

Emma pulled away and spun on her heels to see what had Amy in shock.

Amy jabbed Emma in the ribs with her elbow. "Who's with Dad?"

Emma flinched from the poke in the ribs and waved for them to join them at the beach. "I don't know. Dad didn't say anything to me about bringing someone." She shot Amy a sideward glance. "I can't imagine why."

Amy jabbed Emma in the ribs again. "I'll tell you why. It's because he didn't want us butting in."

Emma's mouth dropped open. "What do you mean *us*?" She shielded her ribs with her hand. "And stop poking me with your bony little elbow."

"Sorry, I didn't realize I was doing it."

Emma draped her arm around Amy's shoulders. "Dad sure looks happy."

Amy's elbow struck again.

Emma flinched. "Amy, if you elbow me once more, so help me, girl."

"Sorry, Emma. I think I know her. She taught at our elementary school. Mrs. Thompson, I think. I never had her as a teacher. I just can't believe Dad has a girlfriend. They look adorable together. I wish he would have told us sooner."

"Why? So you could stick your nose in? Aren't you busy enough with my love life?" A smirk slowly spread across her face. "On second thought, Dad could have taken a little of the heat off me."

Amy absently elbowed her again. "Stop babbling and let's go say hi."

Their father and Mrs. Thompson held hands as they crossed the beach. As strange as the sight was, it was also a relief. She wondered how long their father kept this secret but didn't really care. She was just glad to see him looking so happy.

Their father introduced them like he had done a thousand times before. He stood tall with his chest puffed out. "I am proud to say these are my two beautiful daughters. Emma took after her mother, my Italian princess. And Amy took after her old dad. She is my Irish beauty."

The words felt as good today as they had when Emma was a little girl. She stood a little taller and smiled warmly while shaking Mrs. Thompson's hand.

"It's nice to meet you."

Amy took her hand and didn't let go. She led her toward the picnic table and planted herself beside the woman with no intentions of moving before she had all her questions answered. Amy monopolized the conversation. She wanted to know everything, where they met, how they met, and would they be seeing a lot more of her in the future. Every question imaginable asked and answered. Amy was unable to take credit for the matchmaking, but she would do her best to run things from here on out.

***

Mrs. Thompson excused herself to get better acquainted with the grandchild she had heard so much about. Emma took the opportunity for a little one-on-one and followed her, leaving her very capable father alone with Amy for his round of questioning.

"Thank you for making me feel so welcome. Your sister is still the same sweet girl I remember."

Emma grinned and rolled her eyes. "Is that what you call it?"

"She likes to see people happy, especially her family."

Emma sighed and stared out at the ocean. "My father looks happier than I've seen him in a long time."

Mrs. Thompson rested her hand on Emma's shoulder. "He was pretty worried about bringing me here today. He wasn't sure how his girls would feel about him dating again."

Emma turned her eyes back at her. "We've wondered for years what was stopping him from finding someone to spend time with. Mom has been gone a long time."

"He loved your mother more than words could say. It sounds like she was a very special woman."

Emma eyebrows shot up. "Dad talks to you about Mom?"

"Of course, she was a big part of his life. It comes up quite often when he mentions either of you girls."

"Do you mind him talking about Mom?" She shook her head. "I'm sorry. That is not my business."

She brushed her hand down Emma's arm. "Don't apologize. Your father…he had a life and love before me. That's what made him who he is, and I'm thankful for that."

"Can I ask you a question, Mrs. Thompson? It's kind of personal. You can tell me it's none of my business if you want to."

"Ask away, Emma. And please, call me Debra."

"Okay, Debra. I was wondering how *you* feel, knowing how much he loved Mom, and where you fit in his life, more importantly, in his heart."

"I'm sure you don't need me to tell you that your father is a wonderful man. I believe he has plenty of room in his heart."

Emma cleared her throat. "I should explain. I think I'm falling for someone, and at times I think he may feel the same way. He lost his wife almost a year ago, and I'm not sure where I fit or if I ever will."

"That's a tough one. Only he knows where he stands. All you can do is talk to him."

"Growing up, I watched my parents. They loved each other so much. I want that kind of love."

"There's no reason you can't have it. Time can make love grow stronger every day as long as you nurture it, as long as both of you work for it."

"I never thought of it that way. I guess I just assumed they loved each other from the moment they met."

"I do believe in love at first sight, but that's where the work *begins*, along with all the fun."

Emma scooped up Jessie and kissed where it hurt. Debra came up behind her and put a gentle hand on her shoulder. With the other hand, she caressed Jessie's cheek, wiping away the sand and tears.

"Your father brags about his family shamelessly, and I can see why. He's a wonderful man, Emma, and I'm grateful for his friendship. My husband and I were never friends."

Emma nodded in agreement. "A friendship is important to me, right up there with respect and honesty."

"I couldn't agree more. That is exactly what attracted me to your father. I've fallen hard."

Emma grinned. "Looks like Dad is feeling the same way."

Debra looked smitten as she glanced at Fergus. "I sure hope so, Emma, because I can't imagine my life without him now."

Emma shook her head as she spoke. "I know it sounds a bit ridiculous because I fell for this guy quickly. I tried to stop it, but I couldn't."

Debra smiled and gently touched Emma's forearm. "That's how it happens. When you least expect it, love settles in, and nothing you do can stop it, no matter how hard you try."

"I want love, I want a family, I want happiness, and I am so happy when I spend time with him and his daughter."

"Love finds us in all kinds of places, Emma."

"I suppose you're right."

Debra turned back toward the rest of the guests. "We should get back and help out with lunch."

Emma nodded and smiled. "I'll be there in a few minutes; you go ahead."

She turned back toward the ocean and shoved her hands in her pockets. The water was at peace, gently creeping out with the tide. She squatted and scratched out a few words to her mother in the loose sand.

Thinking of you
needing you
missing you
Love E.

It summed up what she had to say. She knew her mother would be happy her father had found love; it was a shame he hadn't done it sooner. She knew her mother would never have wanted him to spend the rest of his life alone. That was probably never her father's intention. Time had ticked by running the business, caring for his daughters, and putting his own needs on the back burner.

Whatever made her father decide to take a chance on love again was a long time coming. She knew from experience the time frame was different for everyone. How deep, or passionate, or intense the love was made no difference. The time of mourning was as personal and distinct to each person as a fingerprint. Brent may take another month, another year, or another ten years before he was ready to move on. It was impossible to say when he talked so little about what he was going through.

She turned and watched Brent's truck pull into the parking lot. He climbed out and handed Hope the blanket. She ran for the others and scooped Jessie up for a hug. He closed the truck door and made his polite greeting, dropped the cooler at the end of the picnic table, pulled something from it, and held it behind his back as he headed in her direction. She hadn't moved an inch; she just stood there watching.

Brent stood before her. "I owe you an apology, Emma. I know you didn't intentionally put Hope in any danger. I just reacted without thinking. Since Melissa, I worry *so* much more."

Emma raised her hand to cut him off. "Please, stop. I accept your apology. I understand your concerns, your worries."

"I brought a peace offering." He pulled a box of chocolate-covered strawberries out from behind his back. "So, I am forgiven?"

"You are forgiven." She picked one up and turned it around in her fingers. "You remembered."

"Of course, I remember. I also know how much you like walking the beach, so when Amy offered us to join, I figured you'd be in a good mood. More likely to forgive me."

Emma smiled. "All is forgiven."

"Does that mean we can go back to what we were doing?"

He looked so hopeful it pained her to say the words. "It means I will be at the house Monday with the nanny I have lined up. She is wonderful and young and full of energy. I understand she's a pretty good cook too."

"You don't think it's too soon?" His smile had faded.

"Too soon for Hope? No, I don't. I think she's ready or I wouldn't suggest it." She turned to walk away.

He reached for her arm. "I mean…don't you think it would be good if you were around too for a while?"

"I should explain, I think. What happened with Hope, coming to the house every day, staying over, that's not what I do. Don't get me wrong. I care a great deal about all my clients but, somehow, I ended up in a place I never should have been. If I have caused you any hurt or inconvenience, I am so sorry."

"I don't understand, I thought we were…" He paused to choose his words.

"You thought we were what?" Her expression softened.

"I don't know, friends?" He shrugged his shoulders.

"Friends, we are that." She backed away. "We can do lunch once in a while or walk the beach or even just go for coffee, but we can't spend every evening with me at your house doing whatever it was we were doing."

"Can we please talk about this?" He offered his hand. "You don't understand, Emma. I'm doing the best I can."

"I know you are, and I'm sorry if you feel I'm pushing you. That was never my intention."

The lines in his forehead deepened. "That's not it. I mean, I do feel like I'm being rushed, but not by you, just by circumstances." He offered his hand once again. "Please, can we go for a walk?"

She took his hand and squeezed. "I feel like I have no other choice but to step back."

Brent shook his head. "You don't understand, not really. I know you've had your share of grief but not the same as what I'm going through. You can't really understand."

The words cut like a hot knife. She swallowed hard to hold back the tears. "You're right. Maybe I haven't felt exactly what you're feeling, and I pray I never do. The problem is every time I try to start the conversation, I'm shut out."

"Honestly, it feels wrong sharing with you." He let her hand slip from his and turned to face the ocean.

"It's family day. Let's go enjoy everyone." She turned and walked away—and it hurt to breathe.

***

Emma hooked a hand in the crook of her father's arm and gently tugged. "Dad, can I ask you a question?"

"Of course, button, what's on your mind?"

"I've been thinking a lot about Mom lately and how hard it must have been for you. I know how much you loved her, and I know how much you love me and Amy. Why did it take so long for you to find someone? You deserve happiness, Dad, and I can see you are now. I'm glad you found Debra. She's a wonderful lady."

"I don't know why, busy I guess, or I wasn't ready. I'm sorry if I didn't do enough to help you girls find some happiness after the accident."

Emma wrapped her arms around his neck and squeezed. "Don't ever be sorry. You did everything you could. You were sad too, and we made it together, helping each other, just like Mom would have wanted."

He kissed her on the cheek. "I don't know what I did to get you as a daughter, but it must have been something great."

Emma pressed her lips to his cheek. "I love you, Daddy. Does this mean the end of movie night?"

He patted her back like always. "I love you too, button, and I will be expecting you Wednesday night. Bring popcorn."

Amy belted a sleepy Jessie into her car seat and closed the door. She turned to face Emma, beaming like she did when she was little and had a secret to share with her.

"He's in love, sis."

Emma's face twisted like she didn't have a clue what Amy was talking about. "Who? Dad?"

"No, not Dad. Well, maybe Dad is, too, but I was referring to the gorgeous doctor we just spent the day with. It's written all over his face, sis."

She took Amy's hands and sighed. "It's not like that."

"Well, it is for him!"

"Did he tell you that, or are you just saying it because you want it so bad?"

"Don't be ridiculous. You know he didn't tell me. I caught him watching you all day with the cutest little smile on his face. That and I overheard him talking to Mike. You were the main topic."

Emma glanced at Brent. "I guess we'll see. I still have a few more weeks with them."

Amy glanced over at Brent and looked him up and down. "It must be a real struggle keeping your hands off that. I can't imagine him saying no if you tried."

Emma furrowed her brow. "I have no intention of throwing myself at him. If this is going to move forward, it's up to him. I want him to be sure he wants me, and I need complete certainty he's ready, and Hope. Hell, Amy, I don't even know if I can do it."

Amy smiled. "He's a keeper, Emma, they both are, and I'm not giving up."

Emma bundled the collar of her jacket tighter around her neck. "I know it would be amazing to have them in my life, and I have no doubt you will continue to push."

Amy opened her arms for a hug. “I just want you happy.”

Emma stepped into her arms and hugged her tight. “I’m so glad you came. It was a fabulous day.”

Amy spoke while she squeezed her tight. “Me too, sis. See you soon.”

As Amy bent to get into the car, she smiled up at her. “Love you.”

Emma stepped away from the car and blew a kiss. “Love you, too.”

Brent and Hope had already said their goodbyes and were moving toward the parking lot. He had looked back at Emma repeatedly. She watched them teasing and laughing at each other from across the sand, and it brought on a rush of warmth. They had something pretty special going on, and they had blessed her when they let her in for a short period. Her time with them was at an end; it was time to start getting her heart ready for the good-bye. Just thinking about it had the tears pooling. Her heart was splitting in two.

Chapter Ten

All the little things.

As she pulled into the yard, Brent stepped out of the garage and moved toward her car. He opened her door and offered his hand. She slipped her fingers across his palm and swung her legs out of the car. He pulled her to her feet and reluctantly released her hand. "I'm here, like you asked. What time does this nanny arrive?"

Emma leaned her back against the car and crossed her arms over her chest. "She'll be here in about an hour. I wanted the two of us to have a chance to explain what was happening to Hope. It wouldn't be fair to spring this on her."

Brent nodded his head. "Of course, that makes sense." He offered his hand to Emma. "So, we have time for a short walk on the beach."

Emma ignored his hand and shoved hers into her pockets. "Yes, I suppose we do." She stood and walked beside him toward the beach. "I want to make sure she knows that Hope loves the beach and to spend plenty of time out here."

Brent walked beside her, shifting his gaze from the ocean to Emma. "Of course, Emma. I will remind her if necessary."

"I want her to know Hope likes her hair braided for swimming lessons, and she hates jelly, and she is in a deep 'like' for a young man named Brandon." Emma paused and dragged her fingers through her hair, brushing it out of her eyes. "You can't tell Hope you know. It was our secret, nothing to worry a father about."

Brent reached out to brush his hand down her arm, and she pulled back. He looked pained at her rejection, but it was necessary for her own sanity.

He shoved his hands in his pockets. "Good to know, Emma." Brent's eyes dropped to the sand, and he turned and headed down the beach.

Emma moved to follow him. "These things might seem small, but they are important to Hope."

Brent stopped and spun to face her. "I know they're important. All the little things in life are. When you add up all the little things, it becomes something you cherish. Suddenly all the little things are taken away, and that's when you realize how valuable they all were."

Emma grasped the sleeve of his jacket as he tried to walk away. "Are you talking about Hope or is this about Melissa?" She tried to get him to look her in the eye. "Brent, please, I'm here, listening."

He avoided her eyes. It was as though he were hiding something. He gazed out at the horizon. "If I thought it would change anything, I would tell you everything."

Emma's voice bordered on pleading. "How can you know it won't change whatever it is you're hoping for?"

Brent pulled back and turned his back to Emma. "I just know."

Emma softened her tone. "Maybe we should just get back to what we need to do for Hope."

"Maybe you should stay longer. I don't see why you have to end this. Everything was working the way it was." He kept his back to her.

Emma was glad he couldn't see her. She was certain if he turned to her now, he would know she was dying inside. When she left here today knowing the nanny was taking her place, she would be leaving her heart here, as much with Hope as with Brent. It was tearing her apart, and she couldn't tell which of the two mattered most.

"I can't stay forever; that's not how it works. You know that. Hope doesn't need me anymore." It came out as more of a question that she had intended. "Tell me I'm wrong."

Silence hung thick as fog. She waited, holding her breath, praying for the answer that would make her heart soar. He didn't turn around; he didn't speak. He stood like a statue staring out at the ocean.

Emma turned and started back toward the house, clinging desperately to what little control she had left. All it would have taken was a few words, a few simple words to turn everything around.

Brent called after her, "Emma, wait." He jogged to catch up. "I'll walk back with you."

They walked in silence. The man of her dreams only inches away, but his heart couldn't be further. There was nothing else to say.

Hope jumped from the last step of the bus and snuggled into her father's chest. "Daddy, how come you're here?"

He kissed her forehead and held her at arm's length. "I miss you and Emma, and I had something we wanted to talk to you about."

Hope grasped Emma's hand and locked on to her father's with the other. "Okay."

Emma lifted her hand and patted Hope's back. "I have a surprise for you, someone I want you to meet. She'll be here in about ten minutes. Her name is Kayla, and she's a nanny. She is looking forward to spending time with you."

Hope smiled up at Emma. "Okay, I guess. So, she's going to come and be with you and me and Daddy?"

Emma tucked her hair behind her ear, took a deep breath, and eased it out slowly, buying time to choose her words carefully. "I also wanted to talk to you about how much I enjoyed our time together. Hope, you know how we talked at first about how I would be here until you started to feel better?"

Hope nodded her head.

Emma continued, "And how I help other kids who have lost someone they love?"

She nodded again.

"I think you're doing so good, it's time for me to move on to the next little girl or boy who needs my help."

Hope let go of her father and clung to Emma

with both hands. "But you're still going to come here too."

Emma brushed her hand down Hope's cheek. "You can call me when you need to. I'm here for you, Hope. I think you will really like Kayla. She's a wonderful nanny. My job is to help when people are very sad, and Kayla's job is to care for children, families."

Hope tightened her grip. "Emma, you can't go." She spun her head around to look at Brent. "Daddy, you can't let Emma go. Make her stay. Please, Daddy?"

Brent pulled his shoulders up around his ears. "Hope, you know I can't do that. It's not that simple. Emma has a life, and it's time we let her get back to it." He glanced at Emma with pleading eyes. "Am I right, Emma?"

Emma was thankful for the small yellow sports car that pulled into the driveway. She didn't want to answer any more questions. She just wanted to get this meeting over and go home. It felt like a hammer was chipping away at her heart with each passing minute, waiting for the last blow when she pulled out of the yard.

The nanny waved a slender arm in the air to say hello. Her hair twisted in the breeze, and she tossed her head back, sending it flowing back over her shoulder. The bright pink sweatshirt clung to her full breast and molded its way down and over her slim waist. Emma had told her to dress for the beach, and here she was casually walking toward them looking like she just stepped out of a sports magazine.

Hope had moved beside Emma, standing so close she kept stepping on Emma's feet. Brent had moved in behind them both, with his hands shoved in his pockets.

Emma reached out a hand. "Hello, Kayla. I'm so glad you could make it. We've been waiting for you." She tenderly rested her hand on Hope's shoulders. "I was just telling Hope that you would like to meet her today."

Kayla extended a hand toward Hope. "It's nice to meet you, Hope."

Hope took her hand only for a second and then pulled away. "It's nice to meet you, too."

Kayla flashed a big smile at Brent and offered him her hand. "Brent, is it?"

Brent reached around Emma, pressing into her back, and took Kayla's hand no longer than Hope had. "Yes, yes, it is. It's good to meet you. Emma has filled me in on your credentials. You come highly recommended."

There was a slight chill in his voice. Emma could hear it, but she doubted Kayla could. She had no idea what the chill was all about and had no intention of asking, either.

Kayla turned her attention back to Hope. "You sure live in a beautiful place, Hope. Maybe you could show me around."

Emma nudged her by the shoulders. "That sounds like a great idea. Give me a hug before you go. I will see you very soon."

Hope shrugged her shoulders and turned to look at Brent. "I can show you the beach. But you don't have to stay, because Daddy is going to tell Emma he loves her, and *she* is going to stay." She turned and marched off with Kayla.

Kayla looked back, raising her eyebrows in wonder. Emma smiled to put her mind at ease.

Emma took a step forward, and Brent grabbed her wrist. "Emma, you're not leaving now, are you?"

She let him hold her wrist. She didn't have the strength to pull away. Tears welled in her eyes, and her throat was close to choking off any words. "Brent. Please, I have to go…now."

He let his fingers drop to her hand, and he squeezed again. "You could stay…you should stay…for Hope."

Emma tugged her hand free. "Hope will be fine. Kayla is wonderful, and in a few days, she will have everything running smoothly." She turned and briskly moved for her car, calling back over her shoulder. "Tell Hope she can call me later or when she needs to. I'll stop by in a few days after school to check in."

She dropped to the seat of the car and shut the door, shoved the keys in the ignition, and started the car. She wouldn't look at him; she couldn't. She could feel his eyes on her. It was over, whatever *it* was. A violent sob rocked her entire body as her heart shattered into a million little pieces. She spun the car around and fled the driveway.

Chapter Eleven

Love

She felt as though all the color had been drained from her world. While the grey version was dull and lifeless, it held a hint of comfort in its familiarity. A week had dragged by, with Emma stumbling around with her mind barely able to focus on the tasks at hand. Miserable, long, lonely days crammed with memories, dragging into much the same for the nights. She needed to see Hope and make sure the transition was going well. If she stopped by as the bus was arriving, she could hang around for an hour or so and leave before Brent arrived home.

Hope had called her each day to give her an update and repeatedly asked her to come back. She had been reluctant to give Kayla a chance.

She turned into the driveway. The flowers were all gone, and there wasn't a single leaf left on a tree. The last bend in the driveway brought a mixture of relief and longing as the house came into view. The sight of Brent's truck snatched the breath from her lungs. She hit the brakes and considered backing out before he saw her, but it was too late. Brent stepped out of the garage and waved in her direction.

He smiled that sexy smile, the one that flipped her insides upside down. He started toward her car, and with every step, her heart thundered in her chest. A cry of anguish slipped from her lips, but he couldn't hear; he wouldn't know.

He opened the door and offered his hand, a broad smile lighting up his face. "Hello, Emma, it's so good to see you."

More of a croak than a hello spilled from her mouth. She cleared her throat. "Hello, it's good to see you too, but I was actually stopping by to see Hope." She tugged her hand free.

Brent frowned and shoved his hands in his pockets. "Of course. Kayla took her and a few friends to the pool. They'll be back in a few hours." He stepped toward the house. "Come on in and I'll make you a cup of tea."

Emma turned to follow as he pressed his palm into the small of her back. "I can only stay for a quick visit." She stepped through the threshold and slipped out of her coat. She bent and picked up Hope's coat to hang it on the hook beside hers. She picked up Hope's scattered shoes and stacked them on the rack.

"I miss her, Brent. I needed to hear her voice, see her sweet smile. I miss her hugs." Emma felt the sting of tears and excused herself with a trip to the washroom.

She moved down the hall and noticed the walls were vacant of the family portraits except the most recent. A vicious round of guilt stabbed at her chest. Had she rushed him, pushed him too soon? Stepping into the washroom, she closed the door and leaned her back against it to stop the shaking in her legs. Melissa's bathrobe was gone, the book, the reading glasses, all gone. She rubbed her palm across her chest, trying to loosen the band tightening with each breath. Had he moved forward? Was it because of her? Or was it just time? She stepped to the sink to wash her hands and stared at her reflection. If her behavior had pushed him before he was ready, she had failed him and Hope.

A soft knock at the door. "Emma, you okay?"

"I'm fine, thank you. Be out in a minute." She cupped her hands under the cold water and splashed her face. Her hands were shaking, her stomach in knots. Did she step outside the door and tell him how she felt, or did she bundle it all up inside and run for her life?

She squeezed the doorknob, braced herself, and opened the door.

He stood there, his back against the wall, his hands shoved in his jeans, the white t-shirt clinging to his chest, smiling at her. "You want to know what I think about often?"

"Sure, I think." She fidgeted with her hair.

"I think about that first time I met you at your sister's house. How great you looked in those jeans. I think about the way you warm up this house. I think about the time you fell in my lap and how much I wanted to hold you there forever. I think about the walks on the beach and the way you care for Hope and how much she loves you. I think about that day I caught you naked getting out of the tub. Honestly, I think about that one a lot." He dropped his head for a moment grinning like a teenage boy. "A lot." He pulled her little black panties from his pocket, dangling them from his index finger. "I found these in my pocket a few days ago, and I keep thinking about how much I'd like to see you in only these."

Emma reached for the panties and tugged, but Brent didn't release them. She locked eyes with him. "Is there anything else you think about?" She held her breath.

Brent shifted his feet and released the panties. "Do you remember the day on the beach when I said it didn't feel right sharing with you about Melissa?"

Emma shoved her hands in her pockets and pressed her shoulder blades into the wall for support. "Of course I remember."

"I've had some time to think, and I hope it makes sense."

"I'm listening."

"It was me and Melissa. Now all that's left of us is this sadness. If I share with you, then it isn't just the two of us anymore. Hell, Emma. It feels like I'm cheating."

Emma shook her head. "I'm sorry. That doesn't make sense. How does talking to someone about what you're going through even remotely become cheating?"

He stepped toward her, resting his hand on the

wall behind her. His voice was hoarse. "It isn't talking to just anyone. It's talking to you."

"That makes even less sense." She pushed off the wall and started to pass him. "It's my job to listen and help, but if the problem is me, I will help you find someone else."

He grabbed her wrist and held tight enough to stop her. "Stop running away from me."

She spun to face him. "I can't, because if I stay, I'm going to cry, and then you'll know."

"Know what?" He loosened his grip but continued to hold onto her. "I'm not letting go until you tell me."

Her body went limp. "I care about you and Hope so much more than I should. I crossed a line that goes against everything I believe. This isn't supposed to happen." The first hot tear trickled down her cheek. Brent cupped her face and brushed it away with his thumb. His touch released the flood.

Brent pulled her to his chest and kissed the top of her head. "Please don't cry. I've let my heart go somewhere else, too. Not that I had a choice. I didn't. It feels like cheating, not on Melissa but her memory. It's getting easier, when we talk, but it's still going to take time."

She buried her face in his chest. "I'm sorry for all of this, for causing you any pain."

He slipped a hand behind her back. "The only way you could hurt me is by leaving again. I can't watch you leave again, Emma. I want you. I need you like I need my next breath. Tell me you want me, Emma. I want to hear you say it."

She remained silent.

He brushed the back of his fingers up the side of her jaw and circled his finger around her ear. He kissed her neck, and her body sunk into him, his hot breath tickled her ear. "Say it, Emma. Tell me you want me, tell me you love me." He brushed his lips across her ear again.

A soft moan slipped from her lips, exposing her thoughts.

He pulled her against his chest. "I can't move until you tell me. I won't let you go until you tell me to." He tenderly kissed her forehead, then her eyelids. "Emma, please! Tell me what you want. What you need."

Emma gulped in a breath, "What I want…no…what I need is for you to promise me you will love me forever. I need to know I'm not here just because you believe Hope needs me or because I filled lonely nights."

"Emma, my beautiful Emma, I'm more afraid of not having you in my life now than I am of having to face the loss if anything were to happen to you."

She pressed her palms to his chest, feeling his heartbeat racing, his chest heaving with excitement to match hers. Her arms draped around his neck. Her eyes never left his as she inched her way toward his lips.

"I love you so much it hurts. My heart is overflowing, Brent, and I couldn't walk away again without ripping it from my body, because the pain would surely be the end of me."

When their lips touched, Emma wanted to stop time.

"I loved my wife—no, I love my wife; I would do anything to bring her back, but that's not possible. It's time to move forward. The hurt is fading, but my memories of her aren't."

Emma pressed her palm to his cheek. "I would never want you to forget."

Brent tenderly kissed her forehead. "I know, and that's just one of the many things I love about you."

Another tear rolled down her cheek and onto a waiting finger.

"You love me?"

"I love you, Emma, and I want to make new memories with you. I never thought I would love anyone like that again. Since Melissa's death, I've felt a lot of things, pain, regret, guilt…and I worried constantly about Hope. I think my sadness was part of what held Hope back. Then you came into my life, and I started to feel things I never thought I would feel again. You make me want to get up in the morning. You make me smile and laugh, you made me feel love again, and I don't want it to end, ever. You brought all the joys of life back, and now we can't live without you. *I* can't live without you." He leaned in and kissed her forehead ever so softly. Brushing his lips over her cheek, he paused. "I love you, Emma, and every day I love you more."

He reached around her and pulled her close. She leaned in slowly, closed her eyes and, when their lips met, she felt him reach inside her chest and steal every last ounce of her heart.

Acknowledgements

My family, my source of a massive amount of love and support. I couldn't have done it without you. My husband Frank, and three amazing children, Frankie, Johnny, and Lindsay, thank you. My sister Tracy, my good friend Adelle, and my mother-in-law Pat, your words of encouragement pushed me along.

Thank you to my editor, Toni Rakestraw. Your knowledge and patience are greatly appreciated.

Thank you to the Limitless Publishing team.

About the Author

Melanie Adams is loving her life on Vancouver Island with her husband of 28 years. She is continually impressed with the amazing people her children have become. They enjoy as much family time as possible.

Writing has been an undeniable necessity for as long as she can remember. With an imagination on overdrive, the best thing for her is writing.

She loves to read, especially romance and is currently devouring Nicholas Sparks books.

When she isn't writing she is sorting mail at Canada post, usually at some ridiculous time in the morning.

Facebook:
http://facebook.com/melaniea.adams.391

Twitter:
https://twitter.com/@Melanie79035101

Instagram:
https://instagram.com/melanieadams4

Email:
four4@telus.net

Snapchat:
melanieadams52

Join our Reader Group on Facebook and don't miss out on meeting our authors and entering epic giveaways!

Limitless Reading

Where reading a book is your first step to becoming *limitless...*

Limitless Publishing Reader Group

Join today! *"Where reading a book is your first step to becoming limitless..."*

https://www.facebook.com/groups/LimitlessReading/

CPSIA information can be obtained
at www.ICGtesting.com
Printed in the USA
LVHW031439060519
616794LV00001B/338

9 781640 345768